1

LOST

***

a Lavender Lady Mystery

Also by Sherri' Merritt

***

The Lavender Lady Cooks

The Lavender Harvest

LOST

***

a Lavender Lady Mystery

by Sherri' Merritt

For my Father,
who taught me about courage
and the value of work well done.

For the Dutchman,
who taught me to embrace life with
passion.

CONTENTS

Part
ONE

PROLOGUE

FEBRUARY 2004

THE DREAM always starts the same way. I'm at a house party. The house has many small rooms filled with noisy strangers. Jack is at the party too, but I can't find him. I move from room to room searching for him, pushing my way through the crowd as I get increasingly anxious. I know something's wrong, something's happened to Jack, but I don't know what. The rooms get darker as I become more frantic to find him. I trip over someone lying on the floor and wake with a start.

At first, a feeling of dread washes over me as my heart pounds. Then I remember, and the pain is like a knife on a sharp intake of breath. I listen to the insistent tapping of rain on the roof like telegraphic code and lay awake long into the night trying to decipher the message.

***

chapter
ONE

Wednesday, May 21, 2003

Jack and I got a late start this morning with last-minute details for our trip to Alaska on a travel writing assignment. We leave Palisade, Colorado, at 10:30 A.M. and get delayed at Fruita Co-op where we weigh the rig. We're about 500 pounds from maximum at 17,750 pounds! Our rig is a twenty-four-foot Trek motor home towing a Subaru (forty-two feet total length) with bicycles on top and an inflatable canoe stowed below. We possibly got carried away when packing for this trip, but we'll be in several climate zones during the next four months and Jack wants to continue his triathlon training.

We're back on Interstate 70 at 11:45 A.M. and heading for Provo, Utah, for our overnight stop. I spend the day literally wallowing in the passenger seat as Jack and I cruise along at 65 miles per hour. Crossing the Utah desert, we see blooming wildflowers. Later, a few hours from Provo and the terrain changes from desert to alpine mountains. The evergreens and Aspens remind me of home. We reach Provo just in time for the start of rush hour and luckily make it to Lakeside RV park before too long. Happy hour starts shortly after, an early dinner as the air turns cooler, and then we take a walk around lovely Utah Lake before we turn in.

Thursday, May 22, 2003

It's a hiker's breakfast this morning before we pack a picnic lunch. We unhitch the car and head to Bridal Veil Falls for a short hike. There's a lovely bike path along the river that beckons, but today we're headed into the mountains. From Bridal Veil Falls, we ascend a short distance to Sundance where Robert Redford has a stunning ski resort, art school, theater, and a 6,000-acre nature preserve.

The two-hour hike we take from Sundance brings us deeper into the mountains to an amazing place called Stewart Falls. We stand at the base of the falls, which are about twenty stories tall, and our bodies are bathed in glacial mist from snowmelt pouring off the mountain top. It's wonderfully refreshing after a long hike.

We descend back to Sundance Resort and then Provo. As we drive through town, we pass by sprawling Brigham Young University and notice the Mormon temples. This is a clean and prosperous-looking city with lots of development projects in progress.

Back in camp, I try out the tiny RV shower for the first time. A little tricky, but it works great. Dinner and a movie and then we fall into bed. What a great day.

Friday, May 23, 2003

We drive to Uinta National Forest this morning on the edge of Provo with Timpanogos Cave National Monument as our destination. The park ranger tells us the series of three natural limestone caverns is a 1.5-hour hike up a 1,065-foot vertical ascent. After our four-hour-round-trip hike yesterday, my leg muscles are already whining. Jack and I bolster each other's resolve and head up to 11,750 feet and the entrance to the caves. We discover the caverns are well

worth the sweaty, lung-bursting climb—
we may become spelunkers. The first
cave is an eerie wonderland of
stalagmites, stalactites, soda straws,
and helictites. As we're heading deeper
into the second cavern, the lights go out
(accidentally, the guide tells us) and we
proceed with the help of flash lights.
With fifteen people sweeping a cave with
flashlights, it looks like some creepy
disco. What fun!

After an hour-long tour, we
descend back to the ranger station and
return to Provo via the scenic Alpine
Loop. Jack wants to go to the pool for a
swim when we return to camp, but I can
barely keep my eyes open through
dinner. The RV park is full tonight with
Memorial Weekend revelers. The
celebrations continue long after dark,
but we have no trouble sleeping.

Sunday, May 25, 2003

We drive from Provo, Utah to Declo,
Idaho, today, set up camp, and take a
walk along the beautiful Snake River
which flows 400 miles from end to end.
From the riverbank, we watch the

boaters pulling tubers and water skiers skimming across the surface. Our campsite is across from a lovely bird sanctuary and the river. There is lots of bird life we've never seen before, so we put our heads together over the field guide.

Monday, May 26, 2003

We counted 51 pelicans flying in a "V" above the Snake River as we drank coffee this morning. Our drive takes us from Declo, Idaho, to Hagerman, Idaho, where we set up camp. Lots of irrigation farming is here with sugar beets, potatoes of course, canola, peas, green beans, and melons.

Our bike trip to Shoshone Falls this morning is lovely, but the falls are just a trickle as the Snake River Valley is enduring a four-year drought. We pedal past a curious-looking herd of beefalo (cattle bred with buffalo) ruminating placidly.

The afternoon is spent hiking in Malad Gorge with natural springs cascading from the basalt cliffs into the river. Because of the weak economy here, several of the trout farms have closed business, and as a result, 700,000 trout have been released into the lakes and rivers around this area. This is trout fishing heaven and we're tempted to linger for some fishing fun, but the open road beckons us north.

Tuesday, May 27, 2003

We travel the Thousand Springs Scenic Byway along the Snake River from Hagerman, Idaho, to Twin Falls (population 35,000) and spend the day exploring... and practicing Jack's favorite hobby—shopping —not!

In the strange but true category, we discover the dirt ramp where daredevil Evil Knievel tried jumping his "sky cycle" across a mile-wide canyon of the Snake River in 1974. The town folk have erected a monument in his honor here.

Wednesday, May 28, 2003

The forecast today in Twin Falls is 98 degrees Fahrenheit, so we visit the Shoshone Indian Ice Caves where the temperature remains at a balmy 26 F.

Our cave tour guide points out red-bellied lizards and warns of rattlesnakes on the trail to the caves. We're now just outside of Sun Valley, Idaho, where there's still plenty of snow on top of the Sawatch Mountains. After our tour of the caves, we head back to Twin Falls waterfall for hiking along the Snake River. Next time we visit we hope to take in some whitewater rafting. Jack makes wonderful snert for dinner (Dutch split pea soup with ham hocks and sausage).

***

Thursday, May 29, 2003

This morning we head to Bend, Oregon, and as usual, we talk about how soon we will reach the coast. I can't wait to see the ocean again. Today is sunny and beautiful as we cruise Interstate 84 west following the Snake River. We pass lots of farms; then the going is slower as we head through butte country. We stop for lunch along a river and see a snake which we later discover is called a rubber boa, a type of constrictor common here. Lots of sagebrush country flies by our open window before we start to see pine trees. We're just outside of Bend now and heading into a storm. A gust of wind tears off the RV's air conditioner cover and blows it onto the pavement where it lands, breaking into several pieces. After stopping to hastily retrieve the broken cover, the rain finally reaches us; and we drive with the scent of pine and sagebrush washed clean. Our destination is Tumalo State Park, and we see the Cascade Mountains and Mt. Hood snow-covered in the distance. We make camp at Tumalo Park along the Deschutes River as rain continues through the night.

Friday, May 30, 2003

We wake to the sound of rain and notice a wet patch in the ceiling where moisture has seeped in around the now naked air conditioner. Jack sacrifices his rain poncho for a cover and we avoid disaster. Luckily we packed plenty of foul-weather gear.

We hike along the Deschutes River this morning in our rain gear, and by afternoon's sunshine we're exploring lovely downtown Bend, Oregon (population 55,000). We see a film tonight at the outdoor amphitheatre in camp about the Oregon Trail pioneers. Once again, we realize how spoiled we are traveling cross country in our snug little motor home.

Saturday, May 31, 2003

Chilly weather this morning prods us to turn on heat in the RV for the first time. We explore another trail this morning along the Deschutes River, and by afternoon we're headed to The High Desert Museum just outside of Bend. Jack and I are delighted to find this sprawling treasure in the woods with live/interactive exhibits and decide to return again tomorrow.

Tonight we see the final piece of the Oregon Trail pioneer film at the camp's outdoor amphitheater. The stars are bright overhead as the night turns cooler, and we return to our campsite by the light of many campfires.

Sunday, June 1, 2003

It is time for domestic chores this morning while Jack goes on a grueling bike ride. We enjoy a picnic lunch and return to the High Desert Museum for more fun. The weather is sunny with temperatures in the low 80's again today.

Monday, June 2, 2003

We hike to the top of Pilot Butte this morning for a 360-degree view of Bend and the surrounding Cascade Mountains. We see the Three Sisters, Mt. Bachelor, and many other peaks. There's even a peak named 3-fingered Jack which Jack renames 4-fingered Jack after himself as he's lost the pinky finger on his left hand in a climbing accident years ago. This afternoon we hike along the downtown section of the Deschutes River and admire the beautiful park land. There's a driving range complete with a mini golf course close to our camp where we entertain each other, and then it's pizza for dinner and home again to our cozy little RV in the woods.

Tuesday, June 3, 2003

This morning we take one last walk around lovely Tumalo State Park which we've called home for the last few days before we break camp. We make a stop in Sisters, Oregon, for a tourist break and discover a hidden treasure. There's a small grocery store with wonderful delicacies including freshly picked morel mushrooms. Dinner tonight will be slivers of morel, grilled pork, and sun-dried tomato in garlic butter over angel-hair pasta with freshly grated parmesan on top. Heavenly.

Our destination today is Harrisburg, Oregon, as we roller coaster ride through the Deschutes and Willamette National Forests. There are breathtaking views of mountains, lakes, waterfalls, and tall pines as we follow the McKenzie River. This area looks like gardening and fishing heaven, and we agree to come back and explore on our future travels.

We're about an hour outside of Eugene, Oregon, and the roadsides are filled with lush ferns, blooming flowers, and hazelnut groves. We make camp at Diamond Hill RV Park just outside of Harrisburg and have just stepped into "The Twilight Zone."

Our evening walk takes us through the park and down a side road literally swarming with pet rabbits of all colors (we count approximately 100) and mallard ducks and their young (approximately 50). According to the park owners, someone abandoned a pair of pet rabbits along the road several years ago; and since then, rabbits have been happily reproducing and making their home here. Wherever we walk, there are tame rabbits and mallard ducks.

We venture out of rabbit country and hike past a farm house where the farmer is out mowing his lawn. As we pass by on our return back to camp, farmer Charlie hails us and then regales us with stories of his family settling this area. Before we leave, he presents us with three pounds of handpicked Oregon Marion berries frozen from last year's crop and a bouquet of honeysuckle from the hedge in his yard.

Whenever we have met with strangers on our travels, we have found people to be curious about where we are going and where we're from. They are friendly and generously answer our many tourist questions. This is a great country.

Wednesday, June 4, 2003

Breakfast this morning is French toast with fat Marion berries on top. Thank you Charlie!

We bike to Harrisburg (16 miles round trip) and pass fields of rye grass as this is the "grass seed capital of the world," according to billboards. Homes here have calla lilies and Norfolk pine trees in the yards, which I'm used to seeing only in the florist's shops. Later, we stop for tourist information and discover there are more covered bridges in Lane County where we're staying than anywhere else in the western U.S.

We have an appointment with the

Trek RV manufacturer here tomorrow and Friday to have the rig checked from end to end before we head to Alaska. We take care of domestic chores in the afternoon and then enjoy dinner and a movie.

Thursday, June 5, 2003

We spend the day at the service center for Trek (Monaco/Safari) for a complete check-up on the rig. This place is amazing. It's got all the amenities of a swanky resort with laundromat, movies complete with popcorn, a schedule of classes, and a daily lunch-time BBQ party. The staff here have made it as painless as possible for anyone waiting for service on their motor homes.

In the afternoon, we take a tour of the 450,000-square-foot Monaco production facility where the ritzy $$$$ coaches are made. Wow!

Friday, June 6, 2003

Our destination today is Portland, Oregon, where we finish up on motor home maintenance with an oil change and new shocks for our rig at Camping World. We purchase a spare tire mount for the Alaskan leg of our journey and spend the night just outside of Portland.

Saturday, June 7, 2003

We're up at 5:30 for our drive through Portland. The city looks beautiful this morning as we follow along the immense Columbia River where the huge naval ships are in port for the float tours and Rose Parade today. We see barges, paddle wheelers, and yachts lining the river as the city wakes up. We cross the river and enter Washington state. Our destination today is the Canadian border. We have one week left to reach the starting point of our Alaskan adventure.

As we were driving through Olympia, Washington, today on Interstate 5, we decided to stop at the bank for cash before heading into Canada tomorrow. We exited the freeway and were turning all forty-two feet of the rig around in an empty parking lot when we heard a loud pop and a jolt coming from the back of the rig. I jumped out of the coach to see what it was and discovered the tow bar had come loose and jackknifed into the back of the coach with the car attached. Oh no!

As Jack and I are down on hands and knees looking at the twisted tow bar and the damage to the back of the coach, a young man comes toward us. After a brief conference, the young man tells us he will take Jack to a welding shop nearby so that we can get the tow bar fixed. It's 11:30 A.M. on a Saturday in a strange city, and within an hour Jack is back with the tow bar neatly welded. It's a miracle. The damage to the fiberglass on the back of the coach is minimal and the car is unscratched. If the tow bar had come loose on the freeway just five minutes before we exited, it would have been disaster.

Jack decides to put locks on the tow-bar pins so this doesn't happen again and heads off to the hardware store. While Jack's gone, I decide to take a gift of food to the young man who helped us and approach the building he has just disappeared into. I discover it's a church and the young man is the minister here. Thank you, God, for watching over us.

Heading north on Interstate 5, we

pass through Tacoma keeping snow-covered Mt. Rainier to the east of us as we approach Seattle. Bumper-to-bumper traffic through the city allows us both plenty of time to enjoy the city skyline with a beautiful view of Puget Sound and the Seattle Space Needle.

As we continue north of the city on I-5 along Puget Sound, the delicious aroma of smoked salmon brings our noses to the open windows. We make camp at Mt. Vernon, Washington tonight and talk about what we might expect at the Canadian border crossing tomorrow.

***

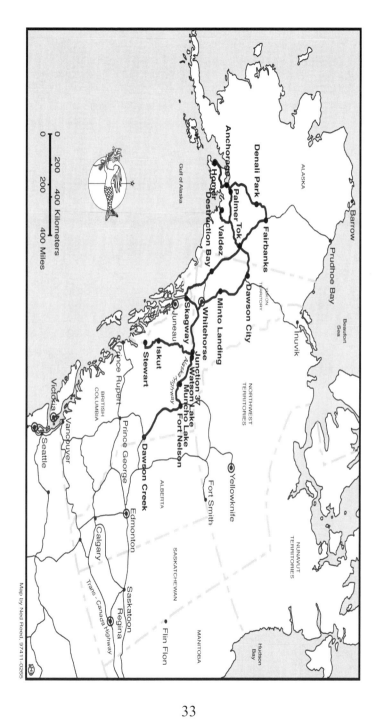

Map by Ned Reed, 97411-0265

Sunday, June 8, 2003

We clear the Canadian border patrol at Sumas, Washington, without incident this morning and head northeast on Canadian Highway 1. Just past Hope, British Columbia, the road becomes a roller-coaster ride through the Cascade Mountains with drop-off views of the Fraser and Thompson Rivers down below. The invisible brake on the passenger's side gets a workout today, and I'm grateful Jack is driving so I can close my eyes when I need to. We see elk crossing signs and lodge names like Caribou and Moose Lake. We even pass a signpost that says Merritt, British Columbia. A golden eagle flying overhead follows the highway with us for a short while as we pass cooling waterfalls along the roadside. We make camp tonight at Cache Creek, British Columbia, where the lilacs are just blooming.

***

Monday, June 9, 2003

We start calculating gallons to liters, miles to kilometers, and American dollars to Canadian. It's 9:00 A.M. as I write this while traveling Highway 97 North, and today we have 325 kilometers to Prince George, British Columbia. Gas is 75.9 cents per liter Canadian (multiply by 3.8 for a gallon!) and our American dollar is worth 1.3 Canadian.

According to road signs, we're on the Gold Rush Trail, the route the gold miners used on their way to the Klondike. We pass semitrailers loaded with logs, some pulling triple trailers of massive logs. The moose-crossing signs become as common as deer-crossing signs at home, and I scan each lake and pond we pass in hopes of catching a glimpse of these long-legged creatures.

The towns we pass through have French and Native American names, and what we refer to as state parks back home are called provincial parks here. We are in the north woods now and pass lots of cottage industries—builders of log homes, fruit stands (selling mostly California fruit right now), many small 10-site RV parks, and even one enterprising soul displays a sign advertising custom wood caskets.

We stop for pie and coffee at William's Lake, British Columbia, while waiting for a rock chip in our windshield to be repaired. Our camp for the night is Bee Lazee RV Park in Prince George where we take a walk through the woods, keeping a sharp eye out for bears, before turning in.

Tuesday, June 10, 2003

We leave our tow car behind in Prince George, British Columbia, for the next thirty to forty days as we continue north on Highway 97. Our destination today is Dawson Creek, British Columbia, which is where we'll join up with our tour group before heading into Alaska.

The Fraser River follows us along our journey through the Canadian Rockies today. We pass hundreds of lakes and rivers, and I am amazed by the endless miles of remote wilderness. There is not a soul on any of the lakes, no houses crowding the shorelines, no boaters, and no one out fishing. Any good hermit would think he had died and gone to heaven here.

As we drive along the twenty-mile shoreline of McLeod Lake, I spot a black bear in a meadow not twenty feet from the roadside. She looks very well-fed.

When we reach Dawson Creek, we stop at the Visitor's Center for information and, as ever, the Canadian people are wonderful and seem truly happy to see us Yankees. The odometer shows we've traveled 2,303 miles to milemarker zero here in Dawson Creek, British Columbia, the jumping off point for our trip into Alaska.

Tubby's RV Park will be our home for the next four days as we get organized for the start of our caravan tour adventure. Here we meet Dave and Arlene from Oregon, co-wagon masters for our tour. We make quesadillas for dinner tonight and take a walk around the park before turning in.

Wednesday, June 11, 2003

We wake to the sound of rain drumming on the roof and spend the morning doing domestic chores, me inside cleaning and Jack with his raingear on outside washing thousands of miles of accumulated dirt from the rig.

Sunshine breaks out of the clouds, and we grab the backpack and head downtown to explore. Five hours later we return to camp toting armloads of groceries.

We play Scrabble with a bottle of wine tonight as we watch the sun set at 9:45 P.M. The days are getting very long now as we get closer to Alaska where we'll have almost twenty-one hours of daylight every twenty-four hours.

Thursday, June 12, 2003

The rain continues today. We give each other haircuts this morning before hiking to the municipal indoor pool to swim laps. The pool is great, and I have the women's locker room and sauna to myself until a dozen eight-year old girls giggle their way through to swim class.

Our stop at Mike's Grill for a delicious lunch by the fire allows us to dry out. We've invited the tour group over for happy hour tomorrow, so we stop at the grocery store to stock up on our way back to camp.

Bill stops us for a chat on our way

in, and then Bud stops by with his Labrador retriever. Bud's a spry 78-year-old man with a twinkle in his eyes. The tour group members are from all over the United States and, without exception, are friendly and excited about heading north into Alaska. I'm the youngest member of our group in years only.

Friday, June 13, 2003

Happy Friday the 13th! It's 9:00 A.M. and we head to the "Crystal Palace" for coffee and a tour-group meeting. This is the Canadian sense of humor in action: The Crystal Palace is really a park shelter with opaque plastic panels in place of windows.

After our tour briefing, we put rain gear in the backpack along with swimsuits as there is a 60% chance of rain again today. We hike to the pool for our daily swim before heading downtown to shop.

We're back in camp by 3:00 P.M. and have a quick nap before we start our party preparations for the thirty-seven people in our tour group. At 5:00 P.M., we head back to the Crystal Palace with wine and hors d'oeuvres and enjoy getting to know our fellow travelers from all parts of the United States. It was another lovely day.

Saturday, June 14, 2003

Today is spent getting ready to break camp tomorrow as we all head north together for the first time as a tour group. The co-wagon master visits us to go over the checklist one last time to make sure we're all ready for our big adventure into Alaska.

During our explorations today, we discover there is a water runway at the local airport for all of the float planes that fly through this area. Amazing.

The Dawson Creek, British Columbia Chamber of Commerce does a presentation on this town of 11,400 in Pioneer Village for the tour group tonight. They are very gracious and prepare a wonderful buffet dinner for us.

This young town was started during World War II when the AlCan Highway was built to protect our remote U.S. territories. Prior to that, the area was inhabited primarily by natives, or the First Nations people as they are referred to here. Owners of small dogs are cautioned to keep them on leashes as eagles have been known to carry them off. Poor Fifi!

We're back in camp by 7:30 P.M. to read the guidebook in preparation for our trip tomorrow. Jack and I are very much looking forward to our big Alaskan adventure, but we have no trouble sleeping tonight.

***

chapter
THREE

Sunday, June 15, 2003

Happy Father's Day, Dad! It's 8:00 A.M., the first day of our guided tour, as we begin the migration of seventeen RV's in our tour group caravan to Fort Nelson, British Columbia—285 miles ahead.

Jack's been voted "official" weatherman and gives the weather report over CB radio to the group before we head out—partly sunny with a chance of rain. It's a pretty safe bet.

We see a herd of bison as we head out of town. Miles and miles of green forest and mountain road fly by, and then the tall lodge pole pines change to black spruce and the forest looks stunted now. We occasionally thump into a frost heave in the paved highway and now see caribou crossing signs. Two gray coyotes are spotted in the roadside meadow, and the guidebook tells us we're now in grizzly bear country. Hikers beware, eh?

We stop at the Visitor's Center in

Fort Nelson before heading to camp where our fellow travelers compare wildlife sightings. Our neighbors saw two moose (why not meese?) and the other neighbors saw a black bear. The Chamber of Commerce does a welcome presentation for us tonight. We're told there are 6,500 people in the entire county encompassing 53,000 square miles with sixteen bears *per person* and only seven Canadian Mounties for protection. The major industry is oil and gas and, because of the muskeg (marshland) everywhere, all of the work is done in winter only when everything freezes solid enough to move heavy equipment in and out of the forest. In winter, the population of this little town swells by 20,000 people hired by oil and gas companies!

Monday, June 16, 2003

Breakfast is local bison sausage and goodies we purchased at the German bakery in town. Oink. Our destination today is Muncho Lake, British Columbia, just 155 miles from here through the northern Canadian Rockies.

The roadside is filled with

blooming wild roses, and I'm pretty excited by the four black bears, a coyote, and herds of stone (mountain) sheep we see today. Ahhh, we reach a beautiful turquoise blue lake surrounded by mountains and discover this is our camp for the evening on Muncho Lake.

A boat ride on the lake narrated by a colorful old sea dog known as Captain Jack this afternoon is a hoot. He points out an eagle's nest large enough for a human body where the female eagle is sitting on her eggs keeping an eye on us as we float by. The lake water is clear enough to see twenty feet down and never gets above 42 degrees F. The largest trout ever caught here was fifty-two pounds!

After our boat ride, Jack and I hike to a nearby lodge for refreshments and return home much later to sit lakeside by the campfire with our tour-group friends. The scenery here is spectacular.

Tuesday, June 17, 2003

It's 7:00 A.M. as we gather for today's tour briefing. The wagon masters keep us awake with lumberjack-sized cinnamon rolls and coffee.

We break camp by 8:00 A.M. and head to Liard River Hot Springs for a soak. The warmth from the hot springs has created a tropical jungle lush with ferns, trees hung with moss, fourteen orchid varieties and many unusual plants including some which are carnivorous. This is an unexpected treasure in remote northern British Columbia.

Enroute to our destination of Watson Lake, Yukon Territories, we encounter another unexpected treat. A mother black bear and her cub are grazing roadside and seem unconcerned as I take their picture, keeping a safe running distance for the door of the motor home.

We drive another five miles down the road and come to a sudden, jolting halt. There is a huge BULL moose standing in the middle of the road just ten feet away from our rig who regards us with calm disdain. I scramble for the camera and snap half a dozen pictures of this gorgeous creature before he finally disappears, loping off into the deep woods in three strides. Seriously folks, the legs on this moose had to be at least five feet tall under his mountainous body and hugely antlered head—topping out to at least nine feet tall. He was magnificent. If we see nothing more on this trip, I can die a happy woman.

We reach Watson Lake, Yukon Territories, early in the afternoon and head to the Visitor's Center. On our way, we stop at the signpost forest and take pictures. There are almost 50,000 signs here from all over the world, and I see many which have been "borrowed" from Minnesota towns. Uff da!

We take a short hike before our tour briefing, and then it's off to the camp office to download email. We've had sketchy phone service since we left the United States, but we're hoping it gets better once we reach Alaska. We indulge in a little rest and relaxation tonight while everyone else heads to the local theatre.

Wednesday, June 18, 2003

It's raining today for our drive to Whitehorse, Yukon Territories, 268 miles away. We pass over the Great River Divide where rivers flowing east from here empty into the Arctic Ocean and rivers flowing west empty into the

Bering Sea.

We stop at the lovely lakeside community of Teslin for a visit to the Tlingit Heritage Center to view the beautiful First Nations handicrafts— beaded moose-hide dresses, carved ceremonial masks, and amazing totem poles, each piece telling its own unique story.

We continue up the AlCan Highway where we weave back and forth between the borders of British Columbia and Yukon Territories seven times on this stretch of highway. I spot what looks like a grouse standing roadside, and what we later learn, is a rare glimpse of the arctic ptarmigan. Jack points out a herd of bison grazing along the road, apparently wild.

Our tour group is treated to grilled steak dinner tonight and a live vaudeville show. There is lots of laughter at this wild and woolly gathering.

Thursday, June 19, 2003

We embark on a bus tour this morning of Whitehorse, the capital of Yukon Territories. We stop to visit the S.S.

Klondike, a paddle wheeler from the 1930's that carried passengers and supplies on the Yukon River stretching almost 2,000 miles to the Bering Sea.

We enjoy a quick lunch with our group before we break camp and continue north to Minto Landing, Yukon Territories. Jack and I stop on the way for a hike down 219 steps and through a thick forest to the shores of the Yukon River at Five Fingers Rapids. Exhilarating. It's potluck dinner tonight once we reach camp with a lovely view of the Yukon River before us.

Friday, June 20, 2003

It's a short drive today to Dawson City, Yukon Territories, a town of 22,000 people that sits at the junction of the Yukon and Klondike Rivers. Once we reach this historic town, we board a bus for a little panning for gold. Jack strikes gold with a nugget almost big enough for us to buy a Canadian liter of gas.

Back on the bus with our group, we head for a tour of Gold Dredge #4, a monster of machinery that ate its way through the gold veins of this area leaving behind what look like huge caterpillar tracks from a distance. Our tour guide, Buffalo, has many stories from the late 1890's when gold was discovered here at Bonanza Creek and started the Klondike Gold Rush. He is accessorized with several large gold nugget rings on his fingers and a large gold nugget tie pin.

We tour the authentically restored town of Dawson City, first by bus and then on foot, before returning to camp for a brief rest. Tomorrow is the summer solstice, the longest day of the year, and so Buffalo returns at 8:30 P.M. to take us up to the top of the Midnight Dome. The view from this mountain top is incredible as we watch the sun dip toward the horizon for just a few hours before rising up into the sky once again.

Saturday, June 21, 2003

We have quite a day today in Dawson City. A walking tour of the city takes us back in time to an 1800's river town. We visit the local cultural center for an Aboriginal Day celebration and enjoy some great music and people watching. We return to camp by late afternoon to change into our swimwear and hike to the local indoor pool for some lap swimming. Later, tour members from Nevada invite us to their coach for happy hour and we catch up with their news.

The wagon master stops by with tales of the first grizzly bear sighting of the trip. One of the tour couples was out hiking in the foothills not far from camp and surprised two grizzly bear cubs on the trail. The couple apparently made their descent very quickly without spotting the mother grizzly. That'll get your heart racing.

It's 9:00 P.M. and time to make our way downtown to Diamond Tooth Gertie's Saloon for the can-can show. We stop by to bring along Bud, a spry 78-year-old from California.

We see people from all over the world who have made their way here for summer solstice celebrations. As we make our way home tonight at 11:30 P.M., we marvel that the sun will dip to the horizon at 1:30 A.M. and return to rise again just one hour later making this the longest day of the year.

***

52

chapter
FOUR

Sunday, June 22, 2003

Everyone is up early this morning to board our motor homes onto the Yukon River Ferry by 6:30 A.M. We say goodbye to Dawson City getting smaller behind us as we cross the river aboard the ferry and look forward to crossing the border into Tok, Alaska, today on the Top of the World Highway. We make the border crossing from Canada into Alaska without incident. It's taken us a month and thousands of miles of travel to get to Alaska. Yahooooo!

A VERY rough gravel road filled with ruts and washboards takes us to Chicken, Alaska. This town is wild and crazy and we stop briefly for a late breakfast that includes reindeer sausage.

It's only eighty-nine miles to Tok as we continue on. The scenery is breath- taking, and then, a view of the Alaska Mountain Range before us. Alaskahhh!

We have an RV-washing party

once we get to Tok, which ends in a downpour with lots of booming thunder. We take a walk in the woods later, and the ground feels like a giant sponge with moss and pine needles soaking up the rain.

Monday, June 23, 2003

Our destination today is Fairbanks, Alaska, population 85,000, the second-largest city in Alaska's interior. We drive through forests of white and black spruce, birch, and aspen as we pass wild bison crossing signs. It's spring here and the wildflowers are spectacular—purple blue lupine, Jacob's ladder, columbine, blue gentian, magenta fireweed, and alpine forget-me-nots, Alaska's state flower. The Alaska Mountain Range is veiled today by a slight haze as last night's storm also brought a lightning fire in the forest near Delta Junction.

Just before we cross the Tanana River, we have our first view of the Alaska pipeline which snakes 800 miles to Valdez. We're elated to spot a female moose with her long-legged baby trotting along in the road in front of us.

Describing these beauties as "babies" is pretty crazy when they stand about four feet tall when born and grow to 1,400 pounds.

Another stretch of beautiful scenery before we both do a double take. It's a female moose with twins grazing along the road just a few feet from us. I scramble for the camera and am so excited I can barely turn it on. Wow!

Another few miles and we reach the North Pole. Yes, folks, there really is a town in Alaska called the North Pole. We stop at Santa Clause's House where we put in a good word for everyone before heading on to Fairbanks.

We make camp just in time for a shower before we're off to Alaskaland for a salmon bake. This is a pig-out feast of grilled salmon, halibut, and Bering Sea cod. I am never going to fit into my wedding dress come September. Then it's on to a vaudeville show at the Palace Theatre. We tumble into bed late with the sun still shining. This was an amazing day.

***

Tuesday, June 24, 2003

We're up early for a 7:30 A.M. tour of the Chena and Tanana Rivers. A huge, four-story paddlewheel riverboat glides us downriver to Susan Butchart's sled dog racing kennels.

Susan is a four-time Iditarod winner and national heroine. She and her husband, David, delight us with a riverside tour of their kennels and a personal look at how she became a champion.

The huskies are very sociable and become barely harnessed pure energy when eight are tethered together in front of a sled. A signal is given and they literally fly around the kennel with David straining with all his might as the sled sends gravel ricocheting at every turn. Someday I'd like to try a sled with maybe *two* dogs attached as it looks like great fun.

We continue downriver to an old Athabascan village where we're treated to demonstrations of salmon filleting and smoking, beadwork, displays of tanned hides and furs, native dwellings, and a wonderful narrative of how life past and present is for this tribe.

As we travel upriver and then back

down, our narrator describes Fairbanks as a gold-strike town (3.77 tons of gold were taken from one creek alone) and now a modern-day boomtown as the city prepares for a natural gas pipeline to be built. We enjoy a wonderful lunch at a restored mining pump house before returning back to camp for a much-needed rest.

Wednesday, June 25, 2003

Our destination today is Denali National Park. We stop in Nenana, a river town on the banks of the Tanana River, for lunch and exploring. We encounter lots of summer road construction today and spectacular scenery with our first views of Denali National Park and Mt. Denali (a.k.a. Mt. McKinley) at 20,320 feet elevation. Temperatures today are in the low 70's with partly sunny skies.

Tonight we have a scrumptious banquet in a wilderness cabin with a dinner show. Ahhh, this is the life.

Thursday, June 26, 2003

Our tour bus arrives at 5:45 A.M. for a

tour in Denali today. With about 22 hours of daylight, there's always lots of activity in the wild.

Today we got to see our first grizzly bears (they're blond here and about 400–500 pounds), a huge bull moose that came right up to the tour bus and curiously looked in generating lots of excitement caught on video, several moose cows with calves, lots of caribou and Dall sheep, a lone female wolf, ptarmigans with chicks, a lovely hovering Jaeger bird, golden eagles, a Gyr falcon, and several marmots. All of this and the spectacular Denali scenery as backdrop. We were fortunate enough to catch a glimpse of the south face of Denali and got a picture before it disappeared under clouds again.

We all returned to camp by 3:00 P.M. tired but exhilarated. This was the best day yet.

Friday, June 27, 2003

Sadly, we have to leave beautiful Denali National Park behind today and head to Anchorage. I would like to return here and spend time hiking and camping in this spectacular wilderness refuge.

As we approach Anchorage, the Chugach Mountains loom ahead of us and then behind as we near the Bering Sea. We make a trip to the Visitor's Center downtown for information on salmon fishing before finding our camp for the night. This is a beautiful city of about 260,000, and we're looking forward to our adventures here tomorrow.

Saturday, June 28, 2003

An 8:00 A.M. tour bus picks us up for a trip to downtown Anchorage. This is a beautiful city in Cook Inlet on the Pacific Ocean. There are gorgeous flowers everywhere and lots of park land. Surprisingly, gas is only $1.59 U.S. here.

Our first stop is a 3D movie, "Alaska the Great Land," with a visit to the earthquake exhibit. In 1964, there was a 9.2 magnitude earthquake that completely destroyed parts of Alaska's coastline with many areas dropping 6–12 feet.

The tour continues to the Saturday outdoor market downtown where we discover many of Alaska's treasures. It's 70 degrees Fahrenheit today and beautifully sunny. Too soon, it's back on the bus for lunch at an old mining camp.

Jack and I continue our tour as many head back to camp for a nap. We visit the wonderful Anchorage Museum; and after several hours indoors, Jack leads me back outdoors, squinting against the sun.

A little shopping downtown makes us thirsty. Time to visit the Sleeping Lady Brewery where we have a 360-degree view of the Chugach, Talkeetna, and Alaska Mountain Ranges and the Cook Inlet. Our waiter points out an amazing view of snow-covered Mt. Denali unhampered by clouds today. We watch shipping traffic glide in and out of the inlet and decide to take a long walk along the shoreline. Luckily, we catch the last bus back to camp at 8:20 P.M. and tumble into bed by 10:00 P.M with the sun still shining.

Sunday, June 29, 2003

Our destination is Homer, Alaska, on the Kenai Peninsula today. Jack and I have been looking forward to seeing this area since the trip started as it is FISHING HEAVEN and Jack is a devoted fan of the sport. We learn that the king salmon are running early this year and are fortunate to be here during this short season.

Just when we thought the scenery before us couldn't get any better, our trip today becomes breathtaking—lush green snowcapped mountains; ice-cold aqua streams and lakes milky from glacial run-off; multitudes of fish camps and lodges devoted to the religion of fishing; wildflowers bursting with color from never-ending sunshine—blue lupines two to three feet tall, white yarrow, daisies, wild geraniums, yellow and purple violets, mountain heliotrope, Indian paintbrush, and magenta fireweed. Our first glacier sightings— massive, frigid, aqua blue mountains atop mountains.

The road follows along the Cook Inlet and we search for spouting beluga whales who come to feast on the salmon. As we approach the Kenai and Russian River areas, we see men and women lined up in the river angling for king salmon (a record 97 pounder was taken out of the Kenai).

We stop in the charming fishing village of old Nanilchik where time has stopped. There's a white Russian

Orthodox church built in 1901 sitting atop a bluff here replete with spire-topped golden domes. Our hike up to investigate is rewarded with another heavenly view of Cook Inlet. This is another great place to spend more time in the future.

We crest a hill and see the long finger of land called the Homer Spit stretching out into Kachemak Bay in the Pacific Ocean. We've arrived at our beautiful home for the next two days.

Monday, June 30, 2003

It's my birthday today and I'm very happy to be here in Alaska with the smell of saltwater and sea life in the air. We spend the day exploring Homer and its beautiful bay.

We start our day with a walk along the beach this morning and a stop in the Two Sisters Bakery for super-sized sticky buns topped with pecans. We sip hot coffee from the large open porch and watch the float planes skim across the water and lift off over the mountains for a day of flight seeing.

We continue our walk along the beach and spot a mother and baby sea otter floating on their backs as they keep us in sight. A lone eagle sits at the water's edge feasting on fish, and just ahead a harbor seal playfully surfaces and dives as it follows us along our walk. I'm delighted to spot loons floating on the briny sea. What a lovely reminder of home.

We have grilled halibut for dinner tonight at Land's End Restaurant before a late stop at the Sawlty Dawg, a local fisherman's saloon where all sorts of colorful characters hang out.

Tuesday, July 1, 2003

Today, we take a bus tour of Homer, population 3,700. This is the halibut fishing capital of the world and we 'ohhh' and 'ahhh' as we see 100-200 pounders hanging on display wharf side as the charter boats return with the day's catch. The smell of smoked fish hangs over the docks as the fisheries are kept busy hauling in salmon and halibut. Our fellow travelers who've returned from their charter trips treat us to stories of their big catches of the day.

We make a trip to the fish market, grocery store, and laundromat today before heading back to camp. We feast tonight on Italian wine, smoked salmon and halibut, fresh cheese, dark sweet cherries and home-baked bread. Yes, I brought the bread machine too.

Tonight we take a cruise out to Gull Island across the bay to see the bird sanctuary. The sea otters and murres (related to penguins) bob and dive alongside the charter boat as we approach the rocky cliffs of the sanctuary where thousands of birds are nesting. The smell is terrific as we coast alongside the cliffs where gulls, cormorants (even the rare red-headed ones), puffins (and the rare crested variety) and murres' nests cover the rocks. A bald eagle makes its appearance and the cries of alarm are deafening as huge clouds of birds take flight. I don't think I could ever tire of seeing this abundance of wildlife. What a wonderful way to end our day.

Wednesday, July 2, 2003

We're up at 6:00 A.M. for departure today. Jack and I take one last walk down the beach to the Two Sisters Bakery for goodies still warm from the oven.

On our return trip to camp, a trio of loons greets us from the water with their haunting calls and a lone eagle sits atop a rock not thirty feet from where we walk. Goodbye Kachemak Bay and lovely Homer.

It's a rainy drive today to our destination of Palmer, Alaska. We make a quick stop in Anchorage for gas and explore Sam's Club before heading on to our camp at the base of a mountain in the Talkeetna Range.

Once we've settled into camp, I give Jack a haircut outside at our picnic table as fellow travelers stop by for good-natured ribbing. We enjoy the last of our smoked salmon and halibut tonight for dinner.

Thursday, July 3, 2003

We're up early hiking this morning through Matanuska Valley forest. Our tour bus picks us up at 12:30 P.M. for a visit to a museum, a reindeer farm (tame caribou), and a musk ox farm—all fascinating. We're back in camp by 4:00 P.M., playing catch-up on chores to *The Very Best of Prince* as I clean and dance my way around the rig.

Friday, July 4, 1003

Happy Independence Day! Our destination today is Valdez, Alaska, the world's most northern ice-free port and nicknamed the "Switzerland of Alaska."

Enroute we see the Matanuska glacier and take a slippery hike/climbing break on the Worthington glacier. The drive today is a roller-coaster ride through several mountain ranges covered in evergreens and aspens. We thump into occasional permafrost heaves which bounce us into the air and back down to our seats again. The permafrost layer can descend to half a mile here.

The valleys glow emerald green in the Matanuska agricultural center as we leave Palmer and pass into alpine terrain with tumbling waterfalls. There are many caribou and moose crossing signs today, but the only wildlife we spot is a Hell's Angel from the North Pole on his motorcycle at a road construction stop.

Evidence of the destructive Japanese spruce bark beetle can be seen here and there in stands of dead trees.

Our route takes us through the famed Copper River fishing country where salmon are jumping out of the water on their spawning migration.

There is an abundance of beautiful lakes and rivers here as we skirt the Wrangell-St. Elias National Park, the largest national park in America and home to the tallest active volcano in Alaska—Mt. Wrangell. The snow-capped peaks are spectacular and the immense wilderness is breathtaking. Mid-afternoon we coast down a mountain descent into beautiful Valdez, Alaska, in Prince William Sound.

Tonight we take a narrated cruise into the bay and discover Valdez' history. The 800-mile-long Alaskan-oil pipeline terminates here and ships in excess of one million gallons of crude DAILY. Tours of the facility were suspended after 9/11 so we hang offshore outside the security zone as the captain of our boat points out the highlights of this engineering wonder.

The original town of Valdez, started during the gold rush of 1898, was leveled during the 1964 earthquake. The survivors rebuilt just a few miles down shore and lived to see the pipeline completed in 1977.

Tragedy struck again in 1989 when the Exxon "Valdez" oil tanker spilled 11.3 million gallons of crude just twenty miles offshore. Sadly, only nine of thirteen animal species that live here have completely recovered from the spill, but the people that remain are optimistic about the future of this lovely place of fjords.

Saturday, July 5, 2003

We explore downtown Valdez and the harbor today. Fishing is the passion here, and there are three fisheries lining the harbor with onsite processing. There are stainless-steel fish-cleaning stations on the wharf that are busy from dawn until dusk.

Jack and I head to the local gear shop for the "hot" salmon lures and to the rental shop for our big salmon rods. This place is a marvelous fish museum with all species of Pacific fish mounted on the walls. I'm hoping not to catch one of the more frightening-looking species like the wolf fish with teeth that look like talons.

We drive the rig just past the salmon spawning grounds and stake out our fishing spot. The pink salmon are running now, and rumor has it that some are catching silver salmon too.

As I'm standing on the shore with the waves lapping at my rubber boots, the fish are literally boiling out of the water all around us. I've never seen anything like this before. The shore is lined with people fishing, and the bay has fishing boats of every size, shape, and color bobbing in the water. We're all here for one thing—SALMON.

Jack catches the first fish within fifteen minutes of casting; it's a great pink salmon. I turn away as he takes a rock and knocks it over the head so that it doesn't die slowly in our fish bucket. For a while, we look like Laurel and Hardy on the beach out for a day of fishing until we get the hang of it.

They don't use bait here, just a lure with a treble hook attached to thirty-pound line, and you don't so much fish as you just try and snag something. We cast and reel and cast and reel as fast as we can.

I slowly inch away from Jack and his "flail" casting method and find my own spot about ten feet away. When one of us yells "I've got a fish!," the other one runs with the net to scoop it up before it flops itself off the hook and back into the water. I catch myself a nice fat pink salmon and say a few words of thanks and apology over it before Jack finishes it off with a rock and plops it into the bucket.

We're standing on the shore looking out over this unbelievable scenery of snow-capped mountains, blue glaciers, sparkling water with salmon jumping, sea otters swimming by, eagles soaring, and gulls crying overhead. I'm having the time of my life slapping mosquitoes and pulling in big salmon in the midst of all of this splendor.

Jack finally drags me reluctantly back to town to clean fish at 10:00 P.M. We've been standing on shore fishing for five hours, and it seems like no time has passed.

The harbor's fish-cleaning stations are a hive of activity as boats are pulling in for the night and happy fishing people from all over the world are busy cleaning their catch of the day. A huge shark carcass sits at the end of our cleaning station ready to be filleted out, and I squat down to take a closer look. This place is filled with wonderful curiosities.

We head happily back to camp with our bags of salmon filets and fall

into bed after a quick shower. This was
a great day.

Sunday, July 6, 2003

We say goodbye to hauntingly beautiful
Valdez and wish you the best of good
fortune in the years to come. Our
destination today is Tok, Alaska, 251
miles away. Tonight we feast on pizza
with the tour group and head back to
camp early for some rest and relaxation.

Monday, July 7, 2003

Our destination today is Destruction Bay,
Yukon Territories, and beautiful Kluane
Lake. The road is very rough and Jack
tests his driving skills today dodging
potholes and washboards.

We pass through Canadian
Customs today for the umpteenth time
and start translating miles to kilometers
and bring out our Canadian currency
again. Our wildlife encounter today is a
black bear on the roadside.

We park our motor home on the
shore of the turquoise lake called Kloo-
on-ee tonight, and our tour group

gathers for a lakeside social with everyone contributing an appetizer. We fall asleep to the sounds of surf.

Tuesday, July 8, 2003

We're headed to Skagway, Alaska, today and the road is winding and narrow with many sharp drop-offs. We're just fifteen miles from our Kluane Lake camp when we stop on the road behind one of our fellow tour rigs. They've spotted a grizzly bear off to the right side of the road. This beauty is brown, very large, and has the telltale hump behind his neck. He is grazing without seeming to take notice of us, and so we take some pictures from the safe open window of the rig. Wow!

We pass through U.S. customs again today and, so far, haven't had any problems at any of the checkpoints on either the U.S. or Canadian side. Apparently mad cow disease and gophers with monkey disease are the worries at this checkpoint today.

We begin our 11.5 mile descent into Skagway with sheer drop-offs on the left. The invisible brake on my side gets another workout.

Skagway looks like the Disneyland of Alaska with a downtown refurbished to look just like it was during the gold rush of 1898. The harbor is filled with three gigantic cruise ships with snow-capped and blue glacier covered mountains as a backdrop. The harbor towns we've visited—Homer, Valdez and Skagway, have some of the most spectacular scenery we've had the pleasure of visiting on this trip.

Jack and I make camp in late afternoon where we wash the rig top to bottom and do laundry. Finished with our chores, we head downtown to explore. We make our way to the harbor where we join a few of our fellow travelers for a lovely dinner and then back to camp for the evening.

Wednesday, July 9, 2003

This is our last full day in Alaska so we're up bright and early to head downtown with the sea of people off the cruise ships. We make a mad dash around all of the shops and then it's back to camp for lunch.

Jack heads up the mountain for a hike and I take myself for a walk around the town. I'm low on energy today from a head cold so I enjoy ambling in the 80 degree sunshine in a Sudafed stupor. Jack returns from his three hour hike and shows me the pictures he's taken to share the hike with me.

Some of our fellow tour members from Nevada have invited us to join them for dinner in the harbor tonight. We take turns in our little cubicle shower getting ready to celebrate our last night in Alaska. Dinner is at the Fishing Company where the six of us have, of course, seafood. We watch the boat traffic in the harbor and listen to the blasts of the cruise ships hailing their passengers to board for the night's cruise.

We return to camp by 9:30 P.M. with our friends, but Jack and I head back downtown to walk off some of our dinner. It's peaceful here now that all of the cruise ship passengers have departed. Skagway is the garden city of Alaska, and we marvel at the huge flowers and vegetables in the gardens growing fat from the almost constant sunshine. We reluctantly head back to camp as we have to be on the road traveling again early tomorrow.

Thursday, July 10, 2003

Everyone is up before 6:00 A.M. this morning to break camp. Jack and I linger in camp after everyone else has departed. We always want to spend one more day in these picturesque port towns and so head downtown for breakfast. Gas at the station before we leave is $196.9 and there's only one pump in town. In Canada it will be at least $2.40 American so we fill 'er up.

With a backward glance at Skagway as we climb over the mountains, I silently say goodbye—for now. I was hoping to linger in Alaska, but Jack is ready to head down the coast into Vancouver, British Columbia, so he pries me loose and we cross the border into Canada behind our tour group. Our destination today is Junction 37 in Yukon Territories, 311 miles away.

More beautiful scenery awaits us today as a small grizzly crosses the road in front of us. She turns to look over her shoulder at us before disappearing into the forest.

We arrive in camp late in the afternoon and finally have an evening to do nothing but relax. We listen to the music of Edith Piaf and talk about the amazing sites that we've seen on our adventure to Alaska. Ahhh.

Friday, July 11, 2003

Our destination today is Iskut, British Columbia 200 miles down the road. We see a black bear cub enroute and stop to see if the mother emerges from the woods. She doesn't show herself after a brief wait so we say goodbye to the cub and head on down the road hoping the cub hasn't been lost.

A few miles later, we arrive upon a truck with camper that has rolled over into the ditch. Thankfully, the four college boys in the camper were uninjured and help has been summoned. The roads here are narrow gravel, and the road shoulders are very soft and slippery. Jack has done a good job of keeping us pointed forward on some very treacherous roads.

We arrive at our camp for the night, a gorgeous mountain resort with a lake. Our camp site is right on the banks of a rushing brook.

After we get settled in, we take a hike to the boat dock and can look straight down to the bottom of the lake

—the water is so clear. I can see lake trout swimming near the dock. We continue our hike around the lake and step over clumps of bear scat. Yikes! There are, as always, more beautiful wildflowers, including an old forest favorite, trillium.

Tonight, we sit by the campfire with our tour group and exchange white elephant gifts amidst lots of laughter. We fall asleep to the sound of the burbling brook outside our door.

Saturday, July 12, 2003

We continue traveling to Stewart, British Columbia today, another 200 miles toward the ocean. We pass marsh ponds thick with lily pads sporting fat yellow blossoms, lots of black bears with cubs, a marmot, snow-capped mountains with lush forests, signs of avalanche with huge swathes of forest snapped off like toothpicks, profusions of wildflowers, wide roiling rivers, beautiful still lakes, waterfalls dropping straight down from sheer mountainsides, beautiful hanging glaciers with warning signs of year-round active avalanche danger, acres of stumps that look like headstones in a forest cemetery from logging, and always fluffy clouds and blue sky with temperatures of 85 degrees Fahrenheit.

We stop for coffee and pie at a heliskiing lodge in the British Columbia mountains. Afterwards, we stroll through the lovely resort grounds marveling at the sod-roofed buildings.

We arrive at our wilderness camp in early afternoon and enter a rainforest wonderland. We're surrounded by tropical-looking foliage and tall pines. The front of the rig points into the mountainside and what looks like a bear cave. A signboard warns of grizzlies and wolves in the area and cautions pet owners to keep a sharp lookout.

Jack and I spend the afternoon exploring the town and board the tour bus at 7:00 P.M. for a trip to the bear fishing grounds. The chum salmon run has just started here, and the grizzlies are coming to fish the nearby river now. This is an amusement park Canadian style complete with viewing bleachers and an above-ground boardwalk for safety. Our patience is rewarded by a grizzly appearance just after 9:00 P.M., but there are few fish just yet so she departs soon afterwards. Our group makes an ice cream stop on the way home, and we head back to camp late.

Sunday, July 13, 2003

We board the tour bus at 8:30 A.M. for a trip to see Salmon Glacier. This is a white-knuckle ride on a wallowing school bus in pouring rain and fog up a steep and narrow mountain road. Our courage is rewarded with spectacular views of a twenty-five-mile long by three-mile-wide glacier. The fog wreaths the mountain top that we stand on as we look down through clouds onto an alien world of deep fathomless crevasses and an ancient glacial ribbon of aqua blue and white.

As we continue on our journey, we pass through Hyder, Alaska, and then back across into Canada and Stewart, British Columbia. We stop downtown on our return to Stewart for a visit to the local bakery. When we get home to camp, we wrap farewell presents and catch up on chores before our farewell dinner tonight at the King Edward Hotel. This is the last night of our thirty-day Alaskan adventure with our tour group and people that have become friends.

Monday, July 14, 2003

It's time for us to say goodbye to all of our new friends in the tour group and to this awesome wilderness country. Jack and I will be making our way back to Prince George, British Columbia, where we'll pick-up our tow car and make our way to Vancouver. From there, we're going to continue our travel adventure down the coast all the way into California. We have been traveling for eights weeks and have covered 6,400 miles. In tribute to this unforgettable nature adventure, here's a quote from Marten Berkman:

"Like temples we built in the past, the earth's wild and silent places are sanctuary."

***

chapter
FIVE

Monday, July 14, 2003

We leave Stewart, British Columbia, and say "goodbye" to our RV caravan tour. What a great group of people. We stop in Gitanyow, First Nations village to view totem poles. Enroute to Prince George, we see aborigines netting salmon on Skeena River, a black bear on the roadside, and many native villages. It's lunch and a shopping stop in Smithers, British Columbia. We dry camp overnight in Houston, British Columbia.

Tuesday, July 15, 2003

It's 9:30 A.M. as we don hard hats for our tour of the Houston Lumber Mill. The technology is fascinating with only one man operating a control center that NASA would be proud of. Next, we tour the Visitor's Center gardens where we see the world's largest fly fishing rod (the fly alone is a foot long) and a beautiful marble fish sculpture fountain.

Wednesday, July 16, 2003

We catch up on domestic chores today with a little rest and relaxation on the agenda for the afternoon.

Thursday, July 17, 2003

We make a service station stop for an air conditioner recharge and then we're off for a little grocery shopping. We return to camp overnight and to pick up our tow car at the Bee Lazee RV Park outside of Prince George, British Columbia. On our wildflower hike from camp, we see ox eye daisies, yarrow, fireweed, Indian paintbrush, and many others.

Friday, July 18, 2003

We depart Prince George this morning with our tow car attached for our destination of Vancouver, British Columbia. We marvel as we pass through Quesnel, British Columbia, with its gorgeous, flower-lined streets. It's overnight dry camping tonight outside of Lillooet, a mountain desert region overlooking Seton Lake Reservoir.

Saturday, July 19, 2003

A hummingbird greets us this morning as we sip our coffee and watch the sunrise. Our travels today take us on a treacherous road with 15% grades up and down, mile after mile as we head to Whistler, British Columbia, a spectacular ski resort town.

Today we see sheer drops into a boiling creek, one lane bridges, hairpin turns, evergreens growing straight up from cliffs, shimmering aspen trees, jaw dropping views, snowcapped mountains, alpine wildflowers, black-tailed deer, and grouse. Forest and mountains keep us company and are mirrored in a beautiful lake beside the road.

We stop several times in the turnouts for runaway trucks as our brakes begin to smoke. Whoa Nellie! This is a wild road with road signs becoming black squiggles on a yellow triangle.

As we pass through First Nations villages we see totem poles in front yards denoting clan history. Many new houses are under construction in native villages and some, as Jack says, are under "destruction."

Waterfalls greet our arrival in Whistler where we spend the day exploring this lovely resort town. We dry camp overnight outside of Squamish, British Columbia.

Sunday, July 20, 2003

Our drive this morning takes us through a tunnel of trees overhead, lush evergreen-covered mountains, and blue hue rising from water as mist. We catch a glimpse of Vancouver Island around each twist and turn. There are long piers with boat traffic large and small, overcast sky, and sheer cliffs. The Straits of Georgia bounded by Vancouver are on one side and Vancouver Island on the other—fabulous real estate. Fast-moving ferry boats carry their loads of people and vehicles to and fro. The water color of Horseshoe Bay is ever-changing from aquamarine to dark, fathomless green. We see lush fern and salmonberries roadside. Graceful Norfolk pine and butterfly bush fly by. Vancouver proper and surrounding areas are in a botanical garden setting.

The endless traffic is a sure sign that we are back in civilization, an idea that Jack and I are both resistant to, having just come from the pristine wilderness of Alaska. We've grown unaccustomed to the massive humanity which we find here. It's a startling contrast to the serenity of the back country.

We continue our journey through downtown Vancouver where there are many beautiful fountains and endless glass skyscrapers to maximize the spectacular views. Tree-lined avenues, tall hedges, and trolley-car cables make a web overhead. There is fantastic scenery and fabulous real estate around every turn. We make camp in Delta, British Columbia near the ferry that will take us across to Vancouver Island in a few days.

Monday, July 21, 2003

It's time for domestic chores and rest and relaxation in camp today. We take a refreshing swim in the pool in the afternoon.

Tuesday, July 22, 2003

We load the car and rig onto the early morning ferry to Vancouver Island, British Columbia. The ferry is three stories high with a formal dining room, cafeteria, coffee and gift shop, and lots of seating for viewing. We arrive in the harbor at 11:00 A.M. and make our way to Goldstream Provincial Park in a cedar forest which will be our home for the next week. This afternoon we take a walking tour of Victoria's lovely harbor which is bustling with tourist activity.

Wednesday, July 23, 2003

This morning we take a four-hour bike tour of Victoria and its stunning water views all around on the oceanside trail. We have lunch in the harbor and watch the world go by. This afternoon we take a trip to Craigdorrach Castle sitting atop a hill overlooking this picturesque city.

Thursday, July 24, 2003

We explore Victoria harbor and the downtown shopping areas on foot this morning. I find some great thrift-store shopping, and Jack discovers all of the wonderful bakeries. We meet for lunch at Murchie's, a proper British tea shop with fresh bakery and deli. It's late afternoon before we return to our cedar forest haven.

Friday, July 25, 2003

I take a walking tour of amazing Butchert Gardens today while Jack visits the pool for a swim and takes a bike trip to the farming areas nearby. I've reserved a spot for afternoon tea in the conservatory here overlooking the Italian Garden. I'm delighted by the dainty savories and pastries that accompany the tea and reluctantly leave this splendid place.

Jack takes me to a couple of fruit and vegetable markets in the farming area that he discovered earlier, and we purchase fresh tomatoes, cucumbers, raspberries, strawberries, and foccacia. Dinner tonight is sliced tomatoes, cheddar cheese, and cukes over olive oil-drizzled foccacia with fresh berries for dessert.

Saturday, July 26, 2003

We take a drive to Nanaimo on Vancouver Island this morning for their harbor festival. We wander the shops and stop to watch a contest of kooky waiters and waitresses balancing fully loaded trays and running at breakneck speed across the main street. There is plenty of spilled beer and broken glass for this one. We return to our cedar forest camp in late afternoon and freshen up before walking to the local pub for a relaxing dinner.

Sunday, July 27, 2003

Today is our last day on beautiful Vancouver Island. We break camp in the early afternoon and take a meandering route to the ferry docks at Victoria harbor where we'll spend the night. We make a visit to Store Street for some last minute shopping, stop at a lovely harbor-side cafe for refreshing hard cider, and enjoy a mouthwatering dinner of cioppino at an art-filled restaurant in the harbor. We had a wonderful visit here.

chapter
SIX

Monday, July 28, 2003

We're awakened at 4:30 A.M. by the Immigration officials at the ferry harbor in Victoria who check our passports. We are finally returning to the lower 48 states after a fantastic visit to Alaska and Canada. The Canucks and Alaskans were wonderful. Until next time, eh? For this ferry crossing to Port Angeles, WA, we've separated the car from the motor home to save about $50. Jack and I board the ferry in each of our vehicles, and by 6:10 A.M. we're waving goodbye to grand Victoria and Vancouver Island.

Once we've reached Port Angeles, Washington, we make our way through Customs and take a walking tour of the city. I spot an Internet Cafe as Jack heads to the nearest coffee shop, and I check email and make phone calls to let family know we're back in the USA.

Our drive this afternoon takes us south on 101 where we finally make camp at a heavenly place on the Pacific

Ocean called Kalaloch in Washington. Tonight we sit perched on a bluff overlooking the beach and fall asleep to the sound of the surf.

Tuesday, July 29, 2003

Our hike along the beach this morning at low tide takes us to the tidal pools where we're delighted to find ochre and burgundy sea stars, tube worms, grass green and chartreuse and delicate pink anemones, barnacles, mussels and sand dollars. The incoming tide finally chases us back up the beach for lunch, a nap and more hiking along the beach later in the afternoon. I could never grow tired of this ocean view and the treasures we find along the beach. Ahhh, the heady perfume of salt sea air. Heavenly.

Wednesday, July 30, 2003

We drive to a beach just north of Kalaloch, oddly named Beach #3, to explore more tidal pools. I'm busy collecting sand dollars and feel rich with my pockets full when we return to camp for lunch. We take a bike ride through a cedar forest on an old logging road this afternoon and stop at Kalaloch Lodge for coffee and fresh berry cheesecake to replenish the calories we just burned off. When we return to camp, we head back to the beach for some late afternoon hiking. Jack makes a delicious Indonesian dinner tonight.

Thursday, July 31, 2003

The sound of the surf greets us this morning as we marvel at our ocean view. Our early-morning hike takes us exploring on the beach. We discover two marine biology research crews doing razor clam density studies along the beach and we enjoy talking with them. They seem eager to share their knowledge and generously explain their research. Unfortunately, we'll have to wait until late September or early October before the clam digging season starts. These beauties are as big as my hand, and the researchers tell us the crowd turns out in the thousands for the harvest.

After we return to camp, it's a hearty breakfast and we reluctantly break camp to head south again on

Highway 101. Our destination is Fort Canby State Park on an ocean peninsula. We continue our drive through the Olympic National Forest and arrive in camp by early afternoon.

By late afternoon, we've settled into camp and our beach walk takes us to the North Head Lighthouse and Cape Disappointment Lighthouse with lights sweeping the waves. Along the beach, we spot a dead shark about 5.5 feet long. It's an eerie sight with sunken eyes and gruesome smile. As the sun starts to slide down to the horizon, pelicans start congregating on shore. I count thirty on the beach as more continue to fly in. We spot a Columbia black-tailed deer munching on green growth on the cliff side. A tern flies overhead crying and swooping toward my head. She must have a nest nearby and I'm reminded of the Alfred Hitchcock movie, "The Birds," as there are now hundreds of birds in the air and assembled on the beach. We climb a sand dune to explore a lifeboat seeming to grow out of the sea grass. Weather has removed part of the lettering on the side so it now reads 'hanghai' and we wonder how this boat got to be here from so far away.

As the air turns cooler and the wind levitates the sand, we finally turn around and trudge down the beach back the way we came. There are now hundreds of pelicans on the beach within twenty-five feet of where we are walking. As always, I am awed by the abundant beauty of nature, and we stand watching them watching us as the sun melts into the horizon.

Friday, August 1, 2003

Our bike ride this morning takes us to the Lewis and Clark Center in Fort Canby State Park near Cape Disappointment Lighthouse. We have a great view of the bay and ocean from here. There are lots of boats in the bay this morning for the opening of salmon fishing. We watch the Coast Guard boat darting in and out and learn later they are cautioning fishermen not to venture past the bar into the ocean as the waters are treacherous. This area is known as the shipwreck graveyard of the Pacific.

We break camp after our bike ride and head east on Highway 30 in Oregon following the Columbia River. Before leaving Washington though, we make a stop at a fresh seafood shop in Chinook for Dungeness crabs and smoked salmon for our dinner tonight. We also make a stop in Astoria, Washington, where Jack visits their wonderful maritime museum. I take a quick shower, spiff up the rig inside a little, and relax with a book in hand while I watch the boat traffic glide by on the Columbia River.

We make camp in St. Helens tonight in the Wal-Mart parking lot, visit inside the store for some shopping, and head to the harbor and the lovely restored theatre to see "Pirates of the Caribbean." We sit in the balcony and eat homemade ice-cream sandwiches purchased at the theatre. What fun.

Saturday, August 2, 2003

We arrive on the north side of Portland, Oregon, across the road from the Columbia River this morning. We tend to domestic chores and take a drive to Salty's on the River for happy hour. It's movie night at home tonight.

***

94

Sunday, August 3, 2003

This morning we drive to the Grotto for a tour and explore this lovely garden built into a cliff. In the afternoon we explore downtown Portland, the riverside, and visit the outdoor market. Our last stop in downtown Portland is Powell's, a bookstore that takes up an entire city block and has great books and people watching. We return to our little home near the river for a much-needed rest tonight.

Monday, August 4, 2003

Today we have an appointment at Camper World to have the exhaust system overhauled. While we wait our turn, we tend to business on the computer, make phone calls, and then we move to the customer service lounge for some reading while the rig is up in the air on the lift. This afternoon we take a drive to Woodburn just south of Portland where the outlet mall is. Tonight, we dry camp behind Camper World as the mechanic didn't finish with our motor home until almost 7:00 P.M.

Tuesday, August 5, 2003

We drive to Woodburn again so Jack can have the brakes on the rig checked out. We head to the outlet mall again as soon as they have the rig up in the air.

By noon, we're back on the road and heading for the coast of Oregon. We make camp tonight at the Chinook Winds Casino on the ocean where we enjoy their dinner buffet and explore the casino. We walk along the beach before turning in tonight and enjoy the perfume of salt sea air.

Wednesday, August 6, 2003

Our exploring takes us to Rockaway Beach just north of Lincoln City where we're camping for a few days. We take the scenic drive along the ocean and stop for lunch at a little place on the beach for smoked salmon salad and clam chowder. Just the fuel we need for a hike. Our beach combing takes us to the sea stacks jutting out into the ocean from the beach before we return to Lincoln City in late afternoon after another lovely ocean drive. It's movie night tonight in camp.

Thursday, August 7, 2003

We tend to domestic chores this morning and enjoy sightseeing in Lincoln City in the afternoon.

Friday, August 8, 2003

We take a drive this morning to Tillamook, Oregon to visit the cheese factories there. Our first stop is the blue cheese factory where we sample and purchase wonderful smelly cheese. Next stop is the gigantic Tillamook Cheese Factory. They have viewing windows of each of the areas of production and videos explaining each step of the process. The best part is the ice cream cones and cheese we get to sample at the very end. Eeek! We're starting to look like two fat mice with all of this cheese.

We explore more beautiful coastline to the south and stop to visit the Yaquina Head Lighthouse and hike on the beach. We stop in at the Interpretive Center and get a historical perspective of the area and the lighthouses on this coast.

This afternoon we're in Newport,

Oregon, where we explore the harbor and stop at a seafood shop for more cioppino full of prawns, clams, crab, shrimp, and rockfish. We stop at the wharf to watch the antics of the Stellar sea lions. The males are HUGE. Our harbor walk also takes us past many wonderful murals of the whales and other marine life. We head to the beach at low tide for a soothing walk along endless surf and to explore the tidal pools for colorful sea creatures. Our final stop in Newport is the glassblower's studio to watch them practice their fiery art. We make camp in Waldport with a view of the bay in front and ocean behind.

Saturday, August 9, 2003

Our destination today is Florence, Oregon, where we have mail waiting for us. We stop for a tour of Heceta Head Lighthouse and the lightkeeper's home which has become a bed and breakfast inn. I read the written accounts of guests and newspaper articles on the ghost that inhabits this house. The remoteness of this place and the resident ghost makes this the perfect spot for a bed and breakfast. Oooh, so creepy!

We meander just a little bit farther south and make a stop at the Sea Lion Caves for an amazing view of the Stellar sea lions in the world's largest sea cave. The acoustics inside the cave amplify the noise and chaos of these huge mammals and the smell is terrific. The males can weigh up to 2,200 pounds and love to roar at each other in their continuous turf battles. Wow!

Sunday, August 10, 2003

Today we loll at the beach all day inside the Oregon Dunes National Park. We're nestled among mountains of sand covered in stiff sea grass that rustles in the wind and are lulled into drowsiness by the soothing sounds of the endless ocean surf. This is the life.

Monday, August 11, 2003

After breakfast, I head to the laundromat and Jack to the grocery store. By 1:00 P.M. the rig is cleaned, laundry done, mail replied to, and I can smell bread baking. Time to explore.

While Jack plays with the camera and computer, I head to the harbor for a self-guided tour of the shops. There are many wonderful nooks and crannies to explore here before returning to camp to pick up Jack.

We head to the dunes and beach for a late-afternoon hike to the pier. Low tide is the best time to explore as the beach wears a necklace of sea treasures pushed up by the waves and left behind by a receding tide. We see glistening lumps of clear jellyfish with violet chambers inside, a carpet of broken shells and some lovely whole ones for treasure hunting, bleached and sculpted driftwood, rocks polished and rounded by the sea, kelp strands that look like feather boas, the sloughed-off shells of Dungeness crabs, sand pipers darting up and down the beach on their little toothpick legs, terns and gulls crying and wheeling overhead, wave after wave whooshing up onto the beach and fizzing like soda. We reach the pier and scramble up onto the rocks to see the view. Wonderful. We go back the way we came—a hard climb up over the sand dunes to the car. What a great day.

Tuesday, August 12, 2003

Our destination today is Coos Bay on the southern Oregon coast. We make a stop at the Umpqua Lighthouse and whale watching station. It's a short drive down this beautiful coast on South Highway 101. We stop at the Visitor's Center in Coos Bay for maps and information. After lunch, I make my way to the local library to check email and return to pick up Jack for our afternoon tour of this friendly harbor town.

Wednesday, August 13, 2003

Last night we stayed overnight in the RV lot of The Mill Casino in Coos Bay, had dinner at their massive buffet, and checked out the casino before heading home to bed. This morning we take a drive to Bastendorff Beach where we unload the bicycles for a ride along the coast. We pedal our way to the Charleston Harbor through forest and beach scenery for coffee and a rest at the High Tide Café where we enjoy bay views from their deck.

On our return trip to the beach, we're still a few miles from our car when

Jack gets a flat tire. Eventually, we get the bikes loaded back onto the car and make our way down to the beach for some hiking and exploring. It's another enjoyable day here with temperatures in the mid 70's and lots of sunshine. We continue our drive down the coast to explore Cape Arago Lighthouse. From the Simpson Reef lookout, we watch the sea lions and harbor seals basking in the sun and swimming near the rocky ledges. We make our way back to Coos Bay and stop at the farmer's market for some wildflower honey. Tonight I make angel hair pasta with Asiago cheese and fresh salmon.

Thursday, August 14, 2003

This morning we take a drive to Sunset Beach where we part company for my tour of the botanical gardens at Shore Acres and Jack's bike ride down the coast. We meet up a few hours later at the beach and take a scenic drive back to Coos Bay for coffee. This afternoon it's shopping downtown and exploring more of Coos Bay. Tonight we're back in camp at the casino where I make smoked salmon, sharp cheddar cheese, and spinach quesadillas. It's a relaxing evening enjoying good books. Jack is reading a spy novel and I'm reading "Ahab's Wife" which is perfect for our trip on the coast.

Friday, August 15, 2003

Our destination today is Crater Lake National Park. Goodbye Pacific Ocean. We had an unforgettable visit here.

We travel east on Highway 42 to begin our trek inland and eventually back home to Colorado. There are lovely evergreen forests here where logging is king. We trade the scent of the sea for the scent of a cedar and redwood forest. We make camp tonight at Diamond Lake just north of Crater Lake.

***

Saturday, August 16, 2003

It's a biker's breakfast this morning to get ready to pedal the eleven-mile lakeside bike trail. Yes, folks, it's another gorgeous day with temperatures in the upper 70's and more beautiful sunshine.

We stop and talk with a U.S. Fish and Wildlife manager who is doing a count of rainbow trout and Chinook salmon migrating up a creek that feeds into the lake. On our return to camp, we prepare the rig for departure. We enter Crater Lake National Park in early afternoon and make our way to the national forest campground where we pick a site to make our home for the next few days. Once settled in, we take our car and make a driving tour around the Crater Lake rim with lots of stops for pictures.

It's movie night tonight as we just bought eight new DVD's. We always get to treat ourselves when we have full hook-ups. Oh, the little things we've taken for granted in the past, like electricity.

***

Sunday, August 17. 2003

Hiker's breakfast this morning and, yes, another beautiful day with sunshine and temperatures in the low 70's. Of the many hiking trails here, we decide on a six-mile trek to Crater Peak with a 1,000-foot vertical climb. We've been at sea level for so long we're not used to the altitude, but we manage to hobble back to the car in about three hours. Lunch is at the crater's Rim Restaurant, and we chat with a couple who lived in Juneau, Alaska, for fifteen years but now live in Bend, Oregon. I'm always eager to hear stories about Alaska.

We head back to camp in late afternoon for showers, catching up with email, and downloading of photos to the computer. It's movie night tonight with barbecued chicken for dinner.

Monday, August 18, 2003

Our destination today is Klamath Falls, Oregon as we travel through the Winema National Forest. We see forests of tall ponderosa pine before the view widens to ranch and farming lands. We enjoy more sunshine today with temperatures in the upper 80's as we move south. The terrain becomes more desert-like with blooming rabbit brush and sage flying by our open windows.

About twenty miles north of Klamath Falls, we see what appear to be plumes of smoke in the distance. We had heard there was a forest fire that threatened the town's center a few weeks ago, but the fire was supposedly extinguished. We get a little bit closer to Klamath Falls and drive mile after mile through clouds of bugs swirling like mini cyclones: all windows are hastily closed tight! These were the plumes of smoke we had seen in the distance, and it makes me think about the biblical plagues of locust. Acre after acre of vegetation along the roadside is covered with what looks like cobwebs. We see evidence of the fire in the blackened hills as we continue south.

The bug haze eventually clears and the road continues along Upper Klamath Lake and its many wildlife refuges filled with beautiful egrets, herons, geese, ducks, and pelicans. We make our way to the Visitor's Center downtown and talk with the locals about the bugs and cobwebs we saw. They tell us about the midges that hatch at this time of year (little green flying insects) and suspect the cobwebs we saw might be the fire retardant that was sprayed on the surrounding hillsides during the recent fire.

With maps in hand, we take a walking tour of the downtown area and then we're off to the coffee shop to satisfy Jack's caffeine and pastry craving. When we step back outside, the pavement and sidewalks radiate heat and temperatures have climbed to the low 90's. Instead of the bike ride we had planned, we opt for the cool darkness of a movie theatre for a late afternoon double feature. We see "Swat" for Jack and "Open Range" with Kevin Costner for me. What a treat. We return to our rig at 8:00 P.M. with the sun already setting so we dry camp on the secure fringes of the Wal-Mart parking lot for the night. Thank you, Wal-Mart, for your hospitality.

Tuesday, August 19, 2003

We make a quick breakfast this morning and then drive to the local grocery store to stock up on wine before crossing into California today. Wine in Oregon is about thirty percent less expensive than in Colorado.

We hope to make it to Reno today as we head south on Highway 97 and then Highway 89 in California. The terrain for today's drive is mountain desert under partly sunny skies. We make camp tonight in northern Reno.

Wednesday, August 20, 2003

We drive the car from our base camp in Reno to Lake Tahoe for a driving tour. It's another beautiful day with 80 degrees Fahrenheit and sunshine.

Lake Tahoe is awesome and we spend the day exploring its beauty. We lunch at the edge of the Truckee River before continuing our journey around the lake. Jack wants to show me the boat ramp and dock he built here at Sand Bay when he had his commercial diving business. Late afternoon finds us exploring where they filmed the "Bonanza" series. Our visit brings back happy memories of my whole family watching the TV adventures of Ben, Hoss, Little Joe, and Hopsing when I was growing up.

We head back to Reno just in time

for rush-hour traffic. Jack and I still haven't gotten used to the congestion of city traffic after our time in the wilderness. We enjoy a relaxing evening tonight with some Muscat wine.

Thursday, August 21, 2003

Today we celebrate three months on the road in a twenty-four-foot motor home together, and we haven't killed each other yet. This has been an amazing adventure since we left our Colorado home in May.

We awaken to the sound of rain on the roof, and it brings cool, fresh air to this very warm place in the desert. We decide to break camp this morning and continue our trek east and to home. We had hoped to spend another day at Lake Tahoe, but the weather has decided for us. We make a short stop at the Sierra Trading Post Outlet and continue east on Interstate 80 from Reno.

We travel from Reno to Eureka, Nevada, where we camp overnight and wait out the flash flooding all around us. The locals said they hadn't had any rain in over a month and now it was coming down in bucketfuls. We are the lucky spectators of this rare storm. The rain comes sweeping down like fringe on a giant curtain. We watch the immense desert sky fill with an ever-changing storm drama in the swiftly moving clouds. Hot flashes of lightning are followed by the sudden hard thud of booming thunder. During a lull in the storm, we watch a doe grazing outside our window and all is peaceful around us for a while.

Flash flood warnings continue until 3:30 A.M. In the wee hours of the morning, we are awakened by a cloudburst tap tapping and then pounding on our roof, but we remain cozy inside in our cocoon of blankets. Before I fall back to sleep, my mind locates where the rain gear might be hiding in the closet just in case the rig starts to float during the night.

Friday, August 22, 2003

We listen to good 'ol honky tonk blues on the radio this morning, which seems just right for traveling through the wild west. Today we have partly sunny skies as we continue east on Highway 50 through the Nevada desert.

The road is a silvery wet ribbon in the distance and the desert world has been washed clean and glows in the aftermath of the storm. We breathe deeply of the sage perfume all around us and bask in the warming sunshine. A few hours later we notice the fat snowy clouds now have blue shadows of rain held against their undersides. Jack says the road is so straight he could tie off the steering wheel and go for a coffee break while the rig continues driving. Our drive takes us climbing and descending, climbing and descending as we pass through the mountains of eastern Nevada. Clouds change to a seething blue-gray mass as we approach another rainstorm near Ely. We camp overnight in Wendover, Nevada.

Saturday, August 23, 2003

Our destination today is the Lakeside RV Park in Provo, Utah. We're coming full circle as this is the first place we stayed at on our way to Alaska way back in May.

We cross the salt flats and desert lands of northwestern Utah and see the spires of the Mormon church in Salt Lake

City. It's early afternoon and we make camp at Lakeside. It was Memorial weekend the last time we were here and today is very quiet in comparison.

We make a late lunch and loll around camp with not much ambition to go anywhere or do anything. We take a much needed afternoon off to do nothing. Tonight we bring out the wine and play hearts, our favorite card game.

Sunday, August 24, 2003

We enjoy a biker's breakfast this morning before pedaling over to Utah Lake State Park. This area is suffering from a seven-year drought, and the lake has receded by about twenty feet. We have the whole place to ourselves until we meet a couple and their three kids from New Jersey who are renting an RV for their vacation. We all marvel at the snow-white pelicans on the shoreline as we chat about what we've seen on our separate journeys.

A short time later, we're back on the trail where Jack gets a goat head thorn in his tire. Luckily, we find another biker who has a pump for just enough air to get us back to camp. Jack makes tire repairs, and we're again back on the trail along the Provo River.

We return to camp about three hours later and notice there's no one in the pool. We exchange biking clothes for swimwear and bask in the sun after a refreshing dip in the pool. We make a late lunch and take care of domestic chores this afternoon. We hope to be home in Palisade either late tomorrow or early Tuesday.

Monday, August 25, 2003

Our destination today is Green River, Utah and tomorrow we'll be back home in Colorado!!

***

Part
TWO

chapter
SEVEN

Two weeks later, Jack was dead. Lost at sea they said. What a strange way of saying he would never return. *Lost at sea*. As if he might somehow be found again. He was never found. Search and rescue did all they could, but the Pacific Ocean is fathomless. Its gigantic blue maw had swallowed Jack like the white whale had swallowed Ahab.

Friends that we'd made on our trip to Alaska had discovered Jack's love of fishing and had invited him to their boat for an Oregon coast fishing trip. Wedding preparations had kept me from returning with him to the Pacific coast. This trip would be Jack's "bachelor party" before we tied the knot in late September. He had been home just long enough to unpack and then repack for a flight from Grand Junction, Colorado to North Bend, Oregon, and on to Bandon where our friends had rented a home for a few weeks of fishing. Our goodbyes had been brief in the excited rush of travel preparations.

After the tragedy, I learned what

happened on the day they left Bandon harbor, everyone in high spirits for what promised to be a memorable day of ocean fishing. A sudden freak storm had blown up while they were still several miles offshore. They had been distracted by the fever of catching fish and didn't notice the blow coming until it was too late. The very dangerous Bandon bar had closed before they could reach safe harbor. A huge wave had hit them broadside while the captain and his wife were in the cabin below, Ben frantically working the radio as his wife, Maggie, climbed into her survival suit. Jack had been topside trying to keep all hell from breaking loose. Everything had gone bad very quickly.

When the first wave hit, the cabin door had been swept shut with Ben and his wife inside the cabin. The boat listed dangerously for what seemed a lifetime and then righted itself before being hit by yet another larger wave. Jack had been washed overboard with only a life vest for protection. By the time Ben had fought his way back on deck, Jack was gone. They were now in the eye of the storm and it was impossible to see or hear anything in the deluge of water all around and the ceaseless howl of wind.

Ben said "it was like the ocean had turned upside down." They thought they would drown. I could still see the terror and anguish in Ben and Maggie's faces as they haltingly retold the story.

Rescuers had searched for days. It was speculated that Jack had taken a fatal blow to the head either before or after being washed overboard as he was a strong swimmer and no trace of him was ever found. They told me he hadn't suffered. They told me nothing more could be done for him. We were all haunted by his memory.

* * *

In November of 2003, I decided to return to the remote village called Bandon on the Oregon coast in hopes of putting Jack to rest. There was no plan to stay.

One of the locals had asked if I had found Bandon or if Bandon had found me. I guess Bandon had found me. The locals also said that Bandon brought people to it that it wanted. Bandon had wanted Jack too.

For weeks, I haunted the beaches in weather fair or foul, walking endlessly, ceaselessly until I was exhausted enough to fall asleep to the soothing sounds of surf. Only occasionally would I be able to sleep without the recurring dream of searching, always searching for Jack in vain, waking with dread to discover he was gone when I reached for him. I kept no accounting of time in this state of numbness.

I was only vaguely aware of November's passing—staccato rhythms playing on the roof during the night, scents of damp earth and cedar, rubber boots dodging earthworms stranded on pavement, gusts of wind pushing me forward during rambling walks, billowing skies overhead, a dog trotting to greet me proffering soggy paws of affection. Days passed and life continued around me.

By late December, the winter storm season kept the ocean in constant turmoil which seemed to suit my inner life perfectly. The sea and I were as one in our moods. I could walk out into a gale on a remote stretch of beach and rage into the howling wind, salty sea spray mingling with salty tears. I was slowly waking from my dark dream.

***

chapter
EIGHT

Eventually, I sold our beautiful little log home in the mountains and said my goodbyes to what was now nothing more than the flotsam and jetsam of a life with Jack which was no more. With a heavy heart, I watched the Rockies of Colorado recede in my rearview mirror and created a refuge for myself on a lavender farm. I felt a sense of belonging here, as if lovely Bandon-by-the-Sea had thrown out a watery welcome mat. Somehow, I felt closer to Jack here. The spell of the sea was finally starting to work its magic.

As I unpacked what few belongings I'd brought with me from Colorado, I discovered a collection of sea treasures gathered through the years: a starfish from the Bahamas, a conch shell from the Cayman Islands, a bit of coral from Hawaii, and shells from every beach I'd ever visited throughout the world. It seemed that almost every vacation escape I had ever made over the years was to the seashore and that these remnants of the ocean were carried with me to conjure up a whiff of briny sea or the sound of surf when I'd returned to the daily grind of "normal life." It's odd that I hadn't realized until now where I felt most at home.

Many months had passed since Jack's death when a local realtor walked me out into a grassy field one day to look at a piece of property. Without volition, I turned to her and said, "This would make a great lavender farm." And so it did. I decided to reinvent myself and became, of all things, a farmer. I pushed myself into hard labor to forget. Sometimes it even worked.

* * *

My mind returns to the present as I sip coffee, listening to the music of *Over the Rhine* on Jefferson Public Radio. I gaze out across a field of lavender, purple blossoms shimmering in a light breeze at sunrise. With coffee in hand, I step out onto the patio, spicy sweet perfume filling my lungs on a deep breath. I can hear the bees humming to themselves as they tenderly groom each nectar-filled bloom. The scene is soporific, but I have much to do today. KCBY-TV will arrive later this morning to film footage of the gift shop and the start of the lavender harvest for the local news. My helpers will be here shortly as well. Thankfully, the caffeine starts to kick in.

By 7:30 A.M., I'm showered, dressed, and finishing breakfast when the first of my helpers arrives. Danuta is a rare find. We call her Dani for short. Of Russian heritage, she is hard-working and completely over-qualified to be doing stoop labor, but she loves lavender as much as I do and I'm happy to have her. As we're collecting our cutting shears and trug baskets, Cole joins us in the farm's gift shop. Charming and talkative, at seventeen Cole is irrepressibly young and keeps up a running commentary throughout the morning.

We settle into the rhythm of the lavender harvest, each person sitting cross-legged in a row with only head and shoulders showing above a glorious riot of purple blossoms. I'm in heaven.

I give half an ear to Cole extolling the virtues of I-phones, and enjoy the intoxicating scent of lavender, the Zen hum of countless bees gathering nectar, the "thwack" of shears cutting lavender, and our baskets filling with gorgeously fragrant lavender bouquets.

A couple of hours later, an SUV pulls into the driveway with a KCBY-TV logo running along each side. By 10:30 A.M., the filming is complete and my helpers are heading off to enjoy the rest of their day. I make a mad dash into the house to transform myself before opening the farm's gift shop at 11:00 A.M. The Lakeside Ladies Club will be coming for a tour and a visit to the gift shop this morning.

By 11:30 A.M., the party is in full swing. The ladies from Lakeside are in fine form today, all in high spirits, and the weather is superb. We meander through fields of glorious lavender bursting with scent and color and talk about gardening and life on the coast amidst lots of laughter.

Once we reach the gift shop, the ladies are eager to smell, taste, and touch the lavender products filling the shelves; and there is much enthusiasm for our morning's efforts as they marvel at hundreds of bouquets drying overhead in the rafters. They laughingly point to a photo on the wall of me standing on a corner at an intersection, dog at my feet, dressed in overalls and holding a hand-lettered sign that says,

"WILL WORK FOR LAVENDER."

After the Lakeside Ladies depart in a boisterous caravan for lunch in Old Town, I have just enough time to tidy up the gift shop and restock the shelves when I hear the crunch of gravel from a car pulling into the driveway. Returning customers from Gold Beach have brought visitors with them from New Zealand. Children in the group are delighted by the praying mantis, our natural bug control at the farm, as curious about the kids as they are about them. The afternoon passes quickly with many happy travelers visiting the lavender farm on this beautiful summer day.

I'm just finishing up in the gift shop at 4:00 P.M. when the phone rings. It's June from the *Plein Air Artists of Bandon*. We go over the scheduling for their upcoming visit next week as I make a few notes on what to prepare. They'll be here most of the day with their easels set up around the farm, so I'll be making *lavender chocolate brownies to die for* as a dessert for their bag lunches.

***

LAVENDER CHOCOLATE BROWNIES TO DIE FOR

1 cup pecan pieces
1 cup unsalted butter
5 large eggs
8 oz. unsweetened dark chocolate
3-1/2 cup cane sugar
2 tsp. instant espresso
2 tsp. dried lavender flowers, crushed
1 TB vanilla extract
1-2/3 c. sifted flour
½ tsp. salt
½ cup semisweet chocolate chips

Preheat oven to 400 F, butter 9 X 13 baking pan, set aside. Combine chocolate and butter; heat in double boiler until melted. Remove from heat; set aside. Beat eggs, sugar and espresso on high speed 10 minutes. Reduce speed to low; add melted chocolate/butter mixture. Add vanilla. Beat until combined. Slowly add flour, salt, and lavender; beat until just incorporated. Fold in chocolate chips and pecans. Pour batter into pan. Bake 35 minutes or until edges are dry, but center is still soft. Cool on wire rack.

***

After I hang up the phone, I see the stock of lavender spritz is low so I make my way into the kitchen to make more product. As I fill and label the bottles, I ponder what a wonderful surprise this business has been. When I planted fields of lavender, I had no idea it would grow legs in so many different directions. I send up a silent prayer of thanks once again for being able to step out my back door and go to work every day doing something that I love.

I'll be traveling to the Coos Bay Farmer's Market tomorrow morning early to sell lavender products so, after I've finished making spritz, I return to the gift shop to get organized. I select only the lavender products that stand up well to the wear and tear of packing, unpacking, and unpredictable outdoor coastal weather.

As I'm loading the last box into the car, the phone rings. It's the pastry chef from SWOCC's Culinary Institute. Kyle and I have become acquainted through the farmer's market and our love of food. We're both looking forward to the students visiting the farm for a tour in a few weeks. He's hoping to inspire them to create culinary masterpieces with organic lavender. We talk about the lavender chocolate truffles and lavender caramels he's making for an upcoming festival that I'll be doing.

By 6:00 P.M., I have my head in the refrigerator pulling salad ingredients out of the bottom drawer. I toss mesclun greens, organic tomato, ripe avocado, and fresh Dungeness crab meat with a little *raspberry lavender vinaigrette*.

RASPBERRY LAVENDER VINAIGRETTE
Yields 1 pint

1 cup raspberries
1/3 cup lavender-infused vinegar
1/3 cup sugar
1 Tb dry mustard
1 tsp. peppercorns, sea salt, lavender blend
½ cup olive oil
½ cup canola oil
¼ cup grated onion

Puree' raspberries with some vinegar. Add remaining ingredients to blender and process until smooth. Refrigerate.

***

Just as I'm sitting down to dinner, the phone rings again and I'm happy to hear my father's voice. We talk about how the fishing has been as I munch my way through dinner and conversation with phone in one hand, fork in the other.

Later in the evening, I wake sitting up in bed with reading glasses resting on the end of my nose and the book, "The Mermaid Chair," open in front of me. The clock reads 8:30 P.M. I struggle to stay awake and read until 9:00 P.M. and finally give up, rolling over to turn out the light. I'm asleep within minutes. Lavender farming isn't glamorous, but it's never dull.

***

chapter
NINE

Market day starts early with sunrise burning off dew as I nose the car through the farm's driveway gate. The scent of lavender from boxes loaded into the back fills the car's interior, enveloping me in intoxicating aroma as I sip hot java from an insulated cup. The toe tapping music of *Lavay Smith & Her Red Hot Skillet Lickers* accompanies me on the drive up the coast to Coos Bay this morning.

Luck is with me as I find a parking spot a short walk from where I'll be setting up a table today. As I unload boxes from the hatchback onto a wheeled cart, the traffic of Highway 101 roars by as the light changes. A semi double loaded with Paul-Bunyan-sized logs vibrates the roadway as it passes.

As I round the corner pulling a cart loaded with lavender, market vendors toss out greetings as Central Avenue comes to life. Canopies are raised with good-natured banter as everyone spreads out their wares on portable tables and racks.

131

There is an endless bounty of crisp fresh produce, nuts and dried fruits, oven-fresh breads in a dizzying variety, glass jars of jams and jellies sparking like jewels in the sun, lush gardening plants, fresh and smoked meats, and the best canned tuna and salmon right off the boat. Mouth-watering scents of barbecue, Kettle Corn, and lavender mingle amidst the hustle and bustle of commerce.

After I get my table set up and groaning under the weight of lavender products galore, a steaming latte' from the corner deli to ward off the early morning's chill warms my cold hands. The market boasts some of the best people watching on the coast. I sit back and enjoy the show.

Locals and tourists laden with bags of goodies stream by on their first pass through. After loading produce into their vehicles, they return for a second round, many with dogs in tow, enough to fill a dog show. There is a wondrous variety of people and pets.

Buskers fill each corner with song accompanied by guitar, hammered dulcimer, clarinet, and sax. A street party atmosphere ensues as the parade of people and dogs continues throughout the day.

Mandy, a musician friend from Bandon, arrives with her beautiful harp just after 11:00 A.M. The market is in full swing by now, and I'm kept busy exchanging bags filled with lavender products for wads of crumpled money. The sound of heavenly harp music soon joins the scent of lavender as Mandy and I create a stress-free zone in our little corner of the market.

The hours pass quickly as the sun arcs across the sky. By 2:00 P.M., the crowd has thinned and I have time to enjoy just talking with people who stop by to say "hello." Carole stops by to consult on where to plant lavender in her yard and to show me her latest hand-knitted creation. Mitch stops with his Shar-Pei, Coco, to get my *broccoli and cauliflower salad* recipe that he enjoyed at a recent potluck.

***

BROCCOLI & CAULIFLOWER SALAD
Serves 4

*1 pound broccoli crowns, washed, trimmed, and cut into bite-sized pieces
1 pound cauliflower, washed, trimmed, and cut into bite-sized pieces*

Dressing:

*½ cup real mayonnaise
2 tsp. Wasabi powder mixed with water to make a paste
1 tsp. soy sauce
2 tsp. lavender-infused vinegar
½ tsp. grated peppercorns, sea salt, and lavender herb blend
1 Tablespoon water
½ tsp. minced garlic
2 Tablespoons chopped red onion*

Whisk dressing and pour over chopped vegetables in bowl, tossing to coat. Serve immediately. Refrigerate leftovers.

***

By 3:00 P.M., another Wednesday market day has come to a close. It's time to load up the few remaining bits and pieces. Within minutes, I'm rolling the last cart toward the car and waving goodbye to other vendors scurrying to get packed up and on the road before rush hour begins. After a stop at the bank and Cash and Carry for packaging supplies, I point the car toward Bandon and enjoy the music of Eric Clapton for the ride home, musing on another day well spent.

Returning to the farm at dusk, I back the car into the gift shop to unload. There's time to restock the shelves for tomorrow before I get busy in the kitchen making lavender spritz, everybody's favorite product. By 7:30 P.M., with a bowl of leftover spaghetti in one hand, I'm in the office checking email, updating spread-sheets, and listening to my mother's sweet voice on the answering machine. I love you too Mom. 9:00 P.M. finds me blissfully sliding between cool sheets, face washed and teeth brushed. Ahhhh, asleep within minutes.

***

chapter
TEN

A couple of women I met in the
Pageturners Book Club, which I joined
shortly after moving to Bandon, invited
me to take a drive up the coast with
them today. Cecelia, who we call Cece,
and Mary are two smart and funny
women, always full of conversation and
engaged in what's going on in the world.

Our destination is Heceta Head
Lighthouse, but we take the meandering
route, stopping along the way for lunch
and shopping in Florence. It's a
beautiful sunny day with a light breeze
and temperatures in the low 70's, a
great day to be on the coast. We laugh
and talk the whole way, listening to the
music of Holly Brook. These friends are
like a tonic for my grieving heart and
I'm grateful for their efforts to cheer me.

As we pull into the nearly full
parking lot next to the light keeper's
house at Heceta Head, we notice a
figure standing at the upstairs window
and jokingly recall the house is haunted.
Whoever is standing at the window
moves away as we approach the house

and round the corner. As we step up onto the porch, the docent greets us and we make arrangements to take the next tour in forty minutes.

As we start to climb the hill to the lighthouse, I sense someone watching us and glance over my shoulder back toward the house. The figure we saw earlier from the back of the house is now at the front upstairs window. This time there is no mistaking it's a man and he seems to be watching us.

I give myself a mental shrug and return my attention to Cece and Mary, who are discussing the gourmet breakfast served to guests of the light keeper's house bed and breakfast. We love talking about food almost as much as we love eating it, and I soon forget about the mysterious man in the window.

The three of us enjoy an excellent tour of the lighthouse and make our way back to the light keeper's house for an afternoon tour. This is a trip down memory lane for me as Jack and I had first visited Heceta Head together. The day is bittersweet, but I tuck these thoughts away in the presence of the irresistible high spirits of Cece and Mary.

The docent encourages us to sign

the guest book before we ascend the stairs to the bedrooms. After I've signed my name, I flip back to the beginning of the book hoping to see Jack's signature from our previous visit. Unfortunately, a new book was started just a few months ago and I feel a twinge of sadness. On a small sigh, I turn away. It's fun to see where all the visitors are coming from anyway.

From the upstairs bedroom, the front window draws me to a spectacular view of the Pacific coast as I distractedly listen to Mary and Cece behind me chuckling over the tiny dimensions of the Victorian bed for two. Idly, my gaze sweeps the front lawn and the few people standing below. I catch my breath as the mysterious man from earlier turns and looks up to the window. I see his face clearly in sunlight. My God, it's Jack! A gasp escapes me as I press both palms against the window, saying his name aloud in a whisper, "Jack!"

Frantic to reach him I turn, unseeing, toward Cece and Mary's astonished faces and rush past them onto the upstairs landing. As I run headlong down the narrow stairs, the toe of my sandal catches on a tread and

I fly forward, making full body contact with hard stairs and coming to a painful sliding stop, my head pointed downward. I'm momentarily stunned with the wind knocked out of me.

I can hear Cece and Mary pounding down the stairs behind me as someone reaches toward me from below. Everyone is talking at once as I'm carefully lifted from the stairs and conveyed to the nearest sofa.

As soon as I catch my breath, I tearfully tell Mary and Cece that I've seen Jack. By the looks they pass each other, they clearly think I'm hormonal, or worse, and sit down one on either side of me murmuring words of comfort. I try to stand, but a sharp pain in my foot brings me back down with a wince. I must have twisted it in the fall.

"I saw Jack! Please listen to me." I implore my friends to go outside and find him, but they clearly are not sharing my sense of urgency.

To placate me, Mary steps to the window to look out on the front lawn only to report there are two women and three young children on the porch, but no one else. A look of concern crosses her face as she looks at me over her shoulder and lets the curtain drop over the view, returning to sit next to me in solidarity.

An older gentleman, with an aureole of white hair, pushes a flask toward me and kindly tells me to take a sip. Apparently, there's a doctor in the house visiting from South Dakota. With the help of my friends and Bert, the good doctor, I'm eventually calmed down and assured that the haunting setting and my overactive imagination has been playing tricks on me.

Dr. Bert makes sure there are no broken bones, just a mildly sprained ankle, and Cece and Mary finally get me home in one piece physically, but mentally I'm a wreck. I can't seem to get my mind around seeing Jack again only to have him disappear like a ghost. What is happening to me?

* * *

During the night last night, I woke to the muted roar of the ocean calling to me, beckoning, so close now. As my eyes closed toward sleep again, I imagined the waves rolling over and over, endlessly reaching toward shore, reaching toward me, lulling me to sleep.

I returned to my dark dreams.

With images flickering on closed eyelids like an old movie reel, I see my family driving down the long dirt road to Grandma's house for Sunday dinner. It's the summer of 1969 in a small Iowa farming town. My father, mother, older sister, and younger brother are all in the car with me.

As I gaze out the car window, I see the perfectly straight rows of seed corn and soybeans passing by like spokes on a wheel. Dust, soft as flour, creates a momentary fog behind the car and settles back into itself. The sun overhead is hot and the vinyl car seat makes the undersides of my bare legs sweat.

As we approach the two-story, white farmhouse, I see Grandma's garden. It is lush with sweet corn, tomatoes, pole beans, potatoes, onions and, of course, cucumbers for dill pickles —Grandma's specialty.

Dad drives the car to the side of the house so we can enter through the kitchen, the heart of this home, where Grandma greets us all with an ample hug. It's so good to see her wry grin and hear her voice, deepened and roughened by years of hard work, loss, and cigarettes. The kitchen smells of

142

wonderful things baking. Today, Grandma is making her special chicken and homemade egg noodles over mashed potatoes, a carbohydrate feast.

We three town kids are fascinated by this wonderful place that Grandma lives where they raise pigs, cows and, of course, chickens. Since chicken is on the menu today, we all file out to the hen house to "assist" Grandma with her selection. After a choice hen is captured, Grandma takes it fluttering flightless wings and voicing its protest to an open space in the big front yard covered in green grass. As casually as if she'd done it a thousand times before, Grandma securely grasps the hen's feet and flips the hen upside down. She very deftly places a foot onto the hen's neck and, with both hands on the chicken's legs, pulls upward in a strong smooth slide. The chicken's head is now separated from its body. Grandma lets go and the headless chicken frantically runs across the yard to escape—too late.

I wake in darkness with a start and find my heart fluttering rapidly in sympathy with the frantic flight of the headless chicken, pondering the strange mystery of dreams. Am *I* the headless chicken? Have I lost my mind?

chapter
ELEVEN

Early morning finds me groggy from dreaming wildly and feeling bruised all over from my tumble down the stairs the day before. I roll over into the fetal position and gather myself together before opening my eyes to the day ahead, more determined than ever to put the past behind me. On a sigh, I throw back the covers and slide my legs gingerly over the side of the bed, feet to the floor. I must have coffee... so I can think. I hobble off to the kitchen to find some motivation in a cup.

While I wait for coffee to perk, listening to the chug and hiss of steam, my mind wanders and comes to rest on the latest surprise in my life. As I absently stir hot milk into darkly rich coffee, mouth curving in a tiny smile, I think back on how I'd first met my friend, Michael.

After what was considered a decent interval following Jack's death, married friends who were genuinely concerned about my "unnatural" single status and trying to get me back in the game had orchestrated a meeting with a single friend of theirs. Others who were watchful whenever I had a conversation with their mates at social gatherings had encouraged me for their own reasons. And so I acceded to their wishes to quiet their concerns and fears and had agreed only very reluctantly to meet this mystery man.

Dating had changed during the time I was part of a couple. Dispensing with the old-fashioned preliminaries of conversation over a leisurely dinner, my date had suggested over the phone that we meet for coffee. I felt like a used car being put out on the lot with a sign stuck to me that said "low miles, runs good". Perhaps he wanted to kick my tires and take me for a test drive before he committed himself to sharing an entire meal. I had to admit, after having been in a relationship for so long, I was feeling a wee bit rusty when it came to the dating game. Coffee laced with something stronger for courage might be a better idea.

Before Jack came into my life, I had experienced only two previous blind dates. On the first date, I had felt like I was being interviewed for a job. A whisper of thought suggesting I should have brought my resume' and a note from my doctor to speed things along crept into my head during the meeting and was abruptly swept away. After all, I'd promised to keep an open mind and maybe he was just as nervous as I was. That turned out to not be the case.

On my second blind date, the man suddenly lost the power of speech when I shook his hand and introduced myself before we sat down to dinner. Throughout the meal, he was wearing a look on his face like the Disney character, Goofy, when he sees the pretty female dog. The look where the hearts come pulsing out of his eyes and his half-opened mouth wears his tongue like a tie. Needless to say, conversation was almost impossible, and I made a graceful dash for the exit when he suggested making me his dessert.

So there I was waiting to meet Michael, sitting at a scarred wooden table at the Bandon Coffee Café and feeling like a foolish offering to the capricious dating gods. As my hands busied themselves over a cup of tea, my eyes glanced nervously off the few locals parked at tables here and there and to the dusty window advertising "hot coffee." Unknowingly, the word "hot" decorated my face from outside the café window as a man looked in at me, and I caught my first startling glimpse of the person I was about to meet.

The tinkling of the bell over the door drew my eyes toward the entrance and in walked my mystery man. As he walked toward me with a smile on his face, I thought "Holy Mother of God." He was gorgeous, what my nieces would girlishly refer to as "a hunk."

I had just enough composure to stand, smile graciously, and offer a handshake as we exchanged greetings. After sweetly asking if he could bring me anything, and me shaking my head mutely, he walked to the counter to order. Sinking back down to my chair, I surreptitiously noticed he also looked *very* good walking away. I could feel my face flush, my hand tingling from the touch of his fingers, suddenly very warm, almost giddy.

"Get a grip." A little voice inside my head was calling me to attention and I sat up straighter, feeling like a prim school marm as I did so. Taking a few deep breaths, trying not to hyperventilate, I decided to sit back and enjoy the surprising stirrings of attraction by the time Michael had returned to the table.

* * *

The doorbell ringing startles me out of daydreaming with an adrenaline rush. My neighbor, Dixie, is stopping by to make sure I haven't forgotten about making the candied lavender flowers for her niece's wedding cake today. It's a late afternoon wedding in Old Town at the Harbortown Events Center followed by a reception. We arrange to have Dixie pick up the candied flowers at 11:00 A.M. so she can put the finishing touches on the wedding cake she's made. It is time for me to get busy.

After changing into farming clothes and with basket in hand, I step across the patio and into fragrant fields of lavender to gather fresh blossoms just as the sunrise is burning off the last droplets of dew. It's still too early for the wild honeybees to have awakened from their slumber, and I gently shake stems of lavender to move sleepy bumblebees out of harm's way. Furry yellow and black bodies buzz drowsily as I trim around them. When the sun went down yesterday, they fell asleep on the last flower they were collecting nectar from, black legs embracing purple splendor before dozing off.

As I listen to the chorus of Townsend's warblers, purple finches, and tree frogs in the lacy Port Orford Cedars nearby, I bend and snip my way through a row, collecting fragrant treasure. The feral Manx cat that lives in the woods sits serenely watching my progress from a discreet distance. An Anna's hummingbird hovers over my shoulder for a closer look, wings a blur, and disappears into the sea of purple. It's Sunday morning so the sound of traffic is blissfully absent. Off in the distance, I can hear the roar of the African lion at the West Coast Game Park as he wakes to greet the day. I smile, imagining myself in a Garden of Eden.

As I reach the end of the row, basket in hand on my way back to the house, I notice dusty footprints from large, deeply treaded boots on the landscaping fabric. What I see next brings me dropping to my knees, toppling the basket of lavender as I brace myself on either side of a fresh handprint in the dirt. The hand print is large and is clearly missing the pinky finger on the left hand. My breath comes out in a rush on his name, "Jack!"

I'm momentarily stunned, focusing my entire attention on the four-fingered print, trying to make sense of it. Suddenly leaning back on my heels, I hungrily search the landscape, willing Jack to materialize. Pushing myself to my feet, I call out to him. "Jack!"

More questions than answers are rushing through my mind in a torrent. I run headlong, tearing through brush and trees at the perimeter of the property like someone gone mad, calling out his name. "Jack!"

The search is fruitless. Deeply agitated, I return empty handed to the overturned basket of purple blossoms.

Standing with hands on hips, I puzzle over the handprint still clearly stamped into the earth, marking its territory.

The corrosive coughing of the neighbor from the other side of a solid wood fence breaks the spell. As the neighbor continues coughing up a lung in anticipation of the first smoke of the day, remembered music of Jethro Tull's *Aqualung* plays in my head and clears it of disturbing thoughts.

On a resigned sigh, I decide against asking Dixie to come and take a look. I don't want to bother her unnecessarily, busy as she is with her niece's wedding day. A worried frown knits my brows as a feather of thought brushes across my brain. Am I imagining this?

I shake my head as if to clear it of grave doubts about my state of mind and bend to gather the fresh cut lavender stems into the fallen basket. With grim resolve, I return to the house for a shower and a quick huckleberry smoothie for breakfast, moving on auto pilot. The strange mystery is shoved to the back of my mind for now. I get busy in the kitchen making *candied lavender flowers* for someone special on their wedding day.

***

CANDIED LAVENDER FLOWERS
Makes 2 dozen candied flowers

24 fresh cut lavender flowers with four
inch stems attached
¼ cup superfine sugar
1 egg white

*Pick flowers when they are 50% open
and after the dew has dried. Whisk egg
white lightly in a small bowl. Dip
flowers into the egg white. Gently
spoon sugar over dipped flowers to
lightly coat. Set flower stems upright in
florist's foam to allow egg white to dry
thoroughly. Store in a lidded jar.*

The candied lavender flowers dry
in record time with the help of a fan so I
make a special delivery to Dixie and
Bill's house across the street from the
lavender farm. I'm greeted by their
adorable Shih Tzu, Gypsy, and am
invited to stay for coffee. Dixie shows
me the beautiful wedding cake she's
made and we happily discuss details of
the upcoming nuptials over cranberry
orange muffins and coffee.

chapter
TWELVE

Returning to the farm in late morning, I can hear the phone ringing in the office after opening the front door. Michael is calling to see if I want to take a walk on the beach with him before our dinner out tonight in celebration of the Fourth of July. His cheerful voice is like a lifeline back to reality. We both had a light breakfast so I plan a picnic lunch as a surprise, my body humming with caffeine as I search through cupboards.

Pushing disturbing thoughts of Jack firmly to the back of my mind, I fill a picnic basket with marinated assorted olives and goat's cheese rolled in the farm's herbs de Provence blend, plump Medjool dates stuffed with pecans, and aromatic lavender smoked salmon* along with crostini. (*Salmon smoked using dried lavender stems like wood chips on a smoker or grill.) I tuck a bottle of my special *lavender-infused gin* and tonic blend in for happy hour later before dinner.

***

LAVENDER-INFUSED GIN or VODKA

After a visitor to the farm said that he placed lavender flowers into a gin bottle that he kept in the freezer for summer drinks, I tried it. The lavender-infused gin makes fantastic gin and tonics. Lavender-infused vodka in a martini with a twist of lemon is another great favorite of dinner guests to the lavender farm.

*Place twelve dried lavender flower heads into a bottle of gin or vodka. Store in the freezer for at least two weeks to fully infuse the alcohol with flavor before using. Add a fresh lavender flower in each glass for garnish if available.

*I prefer the flavor of French lavender for use in cooking or beverages as it is subtle, not overpowering.

***

I drag a brush through sun-streaked hair and smooth on fresh lipstick before packing the picnic basket, beach shoes, and a light jacket into the car. As I maneuver the car through the driveway gate and onto the roadway, I smile in anticipation of seeing Michael again. The music of Rufus Wainwright's "Everybody Knows" plays as background to my thoughts.

***

Michael is a park ranger at Bullard's Beach State Park just north of Bandon. His work keeps him physically active outdoors and accounts for his muscular six-foot frame and suntanned skin, making his smile stand out in contrast. He is the quintessential strong silent type.

We share a love of books and of nature, and we enjoy making each other laugh. He gets my quirky offbeat humor and I appreciate his wry wit and understated style. His hazel eyes glow when he looks at me, making me feel alive again.

Before we met, mutual friends had related to him how I had come to Bandon and the story of Jack. We never

157

talked about it though. I wasn't ready.

***

With a spring in my step and whistling off key, I step across the leaf-strewn path to Michael's front door after parking in the tree-lined driveway. He opens the door with a flourish, grinning from ear to ear, just as I have my hand poised to ring the bell. My heart does a little rumba as I step across the threshold and into the entryway, hugging him in greeting.

"What have you got there?" he queries, noticing the covered basket in my hand.

"I brought a surprise." Grinning impishly, I lift the lid on the picnic basket so he can see what's inside.

"Oh, I love surprises," he replies with a playful smile, taking the basket and leading me by the hand through the sunken living room.

Nestled on a wooded hillside, there are views of the Coquille River running the length of the house. I admire the sweeping view from a large expanse of windows as we step out onto the cantilevered deck.

While we're removing the

158

contents of the basket onto the cloth-covered table, we catch each other up on what's been happening since we saw each other last. As Michael pulls the chilled bottle of lavender-infused gin and tonic from the basket with raised eyebrows and a smile, head tipped to one side, I nod with a grin and conversation continues as he pours out two glasses.

Later, after we've nibbled our way through lunch, we sit basking in a pool of late afternoon sunshine and enjoy each other's easy company and conversation. As I sit listening to Michael telling a funny story about some campers from Iowa, I notice how his smile reaches all the way to his eyes as they crinkle up at the corners. We had become friends and I was grateful.

After we clear away remains of our picnic, Michael suggests a walk on the beach and takes my hand, leading me back through the house and out into sunshine again. A short ride atop a motorcycle, leaning into Michael from behind, brings us to Bullards Beach. After the engine stops, the sound of surf seems to increase in volume, beckoning us down to the beach as we pick our way crablike over an archipelago of driftwood sculpted by wind and water. We hike north into a freshening breeze, stopping occasionally to admire treasure deposited on the sand by a generous sea. The afternoon passes effortlessly into dusk.

***

The air turns cool as we head back to the parking lot, shaking sand from our shoes before riding into Old Town for dinner. As we cross Bullards Bridge, the metal surface shifting gently under rotating tires, the Coquille River is a darkening satin ribbon on either side. The lights of beautiful Bandon glow in the near distance.

As we pull up to the Boatworks Restaurant, the car next to us disgorges its load of golfers, out for an evening's entertainment, sporting Bandon Dunes logo wear. The Fourth of July revelers lining the river's edge are lighting up the night with their rockets and noise makers.

Once inside the restaurant, we ascend to the glass enclosed second story and are seated side by side overlooking the river and Bullards Beach. We have the best view in the house for the fireworks display scheduled at nightfall from the beach. Votive candles are lit and the lights are dimmed in preparation for the pyrotechnic show.

It's a night for celebration as we raise our champagne glasses in a toast to the blessings of life, sometimes bitter, sometimes sweet. As I set my glass on the table, I glance up and catch our reflection in the window. We look like two lovers sitting close together, bodies angled toward one another. As I watch our reflection, Michael leans toward me and whispers in my ear, sending a frisson of electricity through my body. The waitress arriving to take our order is like a cold shower on warm thoughts.

After we complete the ritual of ordering food, there's a momentary awkward silence between us. This is uncharted territory. The music of Astrud Gilberto croons in the background.

A quick glance at Michael reveals a secret smile as his eyes linger on mine. I feel like melting butter. As he takes my hand, our eyes drop to our linked fingers. The heirloom engagement ring that Jack had given me encircles my finger like a talisman.

Haltingly at first, I begin the story of Jack. Michael listens intently, eyes watching the play of emotion like light and shadow across my face. The story is only briefly interrupted by the arrival of dinner and then coffee and dessert. I tell him everything.

As we're lingering over coffee, Michael asks a few questions before turning me toward him, hands on either side of my face to emphasize his words, and tells me quietly that he will do whatever he can to help. The fact that I haven't scared the hell out of him over my recent "*close encounters with Jack*" brings tears to my eyes. I release a sigh on a shaky breath and say a heartfelt "thank you."

Michael promises to do some checking with a few locals, but he won't elaborate on details as he doesn't want to give me false hope. As the spectacular fireworks show begins amidst "ohs" and "ahs", Michael places an arm around my shoulders and tucks me into his side, making me feel safe for the first time in a long time.

***

Lying in my solitary bed later in the evening, mentally replaying events of the day, I marvel how very lucky I am to have met two such rare men as Jack and Michael. They are both men of integrity, "keepers" my grandmother would say.

Just as I'm making my final turn toward sleep, the ringing phone startles me wide awake. Reaching blindly in the dark toward the persistent jangle, I knock the phone receiver from the cradle onto the floor. Hanging over the side of the bed, I reel in the phone cord with the receiver on the end like a plastic fish.

"Hello?"

"I apologize for calling so late, but I've tried several times before and no one was home. I decided not to leave a message because I wasn't quite sure what to say."

"Oh, no worries. I wasn't asleep yet. Who am I speaking to?" The voice sounds familiar.

"Well, they call me four-fingered Jack."

"*What* did you say?" I can hear the chill in my voice as my heart thuds loudly.

"I saw you at Heceta Head Lighthouse," the disembodied voice replies.

"Who is this?" My voice comes out in a whisper as a sob wells up in my throat.

"I thought you might be able to help me. Maybe I should call back at a better time." The voice is now uncertain.

"Who *is* this?" I am openly crying now.

"I'm sorry. I didn't mean to bother you. I'll call back at a better time."

Tears scroll down my cheeks as the line goes dead.

***

chapter
THIRTEEN

Dawn finds me standing at the back patio door watching the sky turn pink as the sun rises over the mountains to the east. I take a sip of coffee strong enough to make my hair stand on end, brooding over dark thoughts.

Moving without conscious thought, I dress quickly in long pants and long-sleeved denim shirt, sliding into hiking shoes on the way out the door. I need movement to clear my head.

As I pass a fenced meadow, two muscular Fjord horses lift their heads from grazing, their silent regard unnoticed as I stride by, lost in thought. Crows caw and heckle from the trees, black shadows perched on branches. A covey of quail, startled from cover, call to each other on opposite sides of the roadway. The foliage thickens and edges closer on Woods Way.

With no clear destination in mind, I'm surprised to find myself on Lost Lake Trail, moving through rain forest terrain and then sand dunes, placing one foot in front of the other, head down. Pushing myself forward, elbows out in front to protect bare skin, I negotiate through a section of path overgrown with prickly gorse.   Nostrils flare as I inhale the sweet scent of its waxy yellow blossoms.

Emerging from the gorse patch, a sandy clearing opens before me as I turn toward the sound of surf. Rounding a bend, New River sweeps before me, liquid barrier to dunes and ocean on the other side.

As I approach the water's edge, a pair of wood ducks is startled into flight, exclaiming alarm as their wings lift them to safety. Perching atop a massive log scoured smooth and gray, I catch my breath.   Attempting to still chaotic thoughts, I focus on the rushing water before me and the swell of sea beyond. The present moment is surreal.   It's becoming increasingly difficult to distinguish between reality and dreaming.   I seem to be haunted by Jack whether awake or asleep. What is real?

***

The screeching of gulls overhead transports me back to the scene before me. I stand suddenly, needing movement. The sound of surf on the far side of New River lulls me forward. A fallen log provides a precarious bridge across the river now diminished by summer's drought. As if in a trance, I find myself crossing the log bridge like a sleepwalker to the other side. The beach beckons and I find myself drawn to the water's edge, watching the ebb and flow of waves, ceaseless, mesmerizing. I'm momentarily stilled, breathing deeply. I clear my mind of chaotic thoughts, at one with the ocean before me, blue sky above. This is my sanctuary. Peace envelops me. I'd like to stay here forever, just like this. I close my eyes and turn my face toward the sun like a flower, seeking warmth. I breathe deeply once more. Heavenly.

***

Part
THREE

chapter FIFTEEN

"SAMANTHA, wake up!" a voice calls urgently from far away. "Samantha!" The voice closer now, compelling.

I stir, as if from the dark recesses of the deep. Feeling like I have lead boots on, I struggle upward toward the watery light above, coughing awake.

Suddenly, life bursts forth around me, sensation and sound rushing at me from all directions. "She's awake!" a voice calls excitedly. "Oh, thank God!" another voice exclaims, this time a woman's.

When I open my eyes, several anxious faces hover over me while a siren's blaring suddenly registers in my lethargic brain. I'm lying flat on my back in a rapidly moving vehicle, an ambulance, and there's an EMT at my elbow calmly checking vital signs.

There's something strange on my face and a wave of panic washes over me. I reach up and start pulling at the oxygen mask over my mouth. A hand reaches out to calm me, a hand with four fingers.

I stare transfixed at the hand that settles on my own atop my chest. Gradually, as if watching a movie in slow motion, frame by frame, my eyes take in the hand, connected to the arm, and up to the face of the man looking down at me. It's the handsome park ranger, but it's also Jack. *How strange*. Suddenly, everything clicks into place and then goes dark as the shock sends me reeling.

***

EPILOGUE

SEPTEMBER 2004

The mind is a curious and fragile thing. Turns out it wasn't *Jack* who had been washed overboard during a wild storm; it was me. Because of the severity of the gale, it was six long, panicked minutes before they could rescue me. By the time I was pulled out of the cold sea's embrace, hypothermia had set in and finally unconsciousness.

While I was "asleep," my subconscious created a chimera with clicks and cuts from past and present plaited together into a strange dream monster. I was truly lost for a time.

When I finally regained full consciousness in the hospital, Jack was right there by my side where he'd always been. I've been lucky, the doctor says. Post-traumatic amnesia from coma can sometimes take months to recover from. Some are not as fortunate and never fully regain consciousness.

He gives Jack much of the credit for my speedy recovery, who hounded

173

me daily to play Scrabble with him, work puzzles, and talked to me endlessly of the past, the present, and our future together. When my memory faltered, he would fill in the blanks until eventually, the puzzle pieces became a complete picture. He jokingly tells people that I took a trip without him, but I never left the farm.

It's been almost six weeks since I left the hospital and Jack and I are ready for a vacation, our honeymoon. We've decided to get married on the beach in Bandon and begin our life together where it almost ended. Our friends, Maggie and Ben, had offered us the use of their boat for the small, intimate ceremony, but I'm not quite ready yet to venture back out onto the water. I've made peace with the ocean, but I maintain a healthy respect for its awesome power and keep a safe distance from sneaker waves when walking on the beach.

Our honeymoon will take us on another road trip in our motor home, this time back to Colorado for fall color season when the Aspens glow. I look forward to visiting old friends there and seeing our beloved log cabin.

We're planning a longer trip next

summer to the coast of California and have enjoyed putting our heads together over maps and travel brochures during the early planning stages. I think this is also Jack's way of keeping me mentally stimulated and engaged in what's going on around me. He knows how much I long to travel again.

Returning home to the lavender farm has been a tonic for me, as always. Long days spent in the hospital regaining full mental awareness had taken their toll on me physically. Spending quiet days slowly becoming reacquainted with the rhythms of nature and of the physical work required at the farm have strengthened not only weakened muscles, but my spirit as well. I am happy and well and truly grateful.

Long shadows appear reminding me the day is coming to a close and so I end this tale and turn to finish cleaning the motor home in preparation for our next adventure. Sometimes, you have to leave home to appreciate what you left behind— enjoy the journey.

***

Acknowledgements

Many thanks to Dorothy and Dick Dark, good neighbors who've shared their fishing stories and always have the coffee on; Wayne Butler from Prowler Charters who answered my questions about ocean currents and the Bandon bar; to Sandy Oldfield, Mhaire Merryman and Maureen Haggerty for reading a very rough draft of this book; to Cleone Reed for editing and design assistance; to my loyal customers and the good people of Bandon who support my creative endeavors; and to my parents who believe in me.

If there should be any errors or omissions in this work of fiction, the responsibility is entirely mine.

About the Author

Sherri' (*cherie'*) Merritt discovered another way to live upon moving to Bandon, Oregon from the mountains of Colorado. After working in the corporate world and as a small business owner for most of her life, she became known locally as "the lavender lady" after starting an organic lavender farm.

As a small business owner, she wears many hats as a grower, agri-tourism guide, a nursery and gift shop owner, and product manufacturer of a natural line of lavender products sold in the U.S. and Canada.

Sherri' has authored two books introducing folks to lavender, *The Lavender Lady Cooks,* a cookbook and *The Lavender Harvest*, an organic growing guide. *Lost, a Lavender Lady Mystery* is her first novel of fiction.

Sherri' loves stepping out her back door into fields of lavender to work every day. The endless variety of people she meets from around the world and opportunities to create, learn, and grow makes work her passion.

About Merritt Lavender Farm

Merritt Lavender Farm is located six miles south of Bandon on Hwy. 101, right on McTimmons Lane, left at the first driveway. The new labyrinth garden opened for tours in the spring of 2011 and the farm's gift shop is open June-September from 11 A.M.-4 P.M. with free self-guided farm tours. The farm is closed Wednesdays and Sundays. The lavender lady sells lavender products at the Wednesday Farmer's Market in Coos Bay May to October. The farm is open by appointment off season. Please call 541.347.7190 or visit our website at www.lavenderladyfarm.com.